THE MILL DAUGHTER'S COURAGE

VICTORIAN ROMANCE

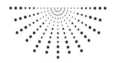

JESSICA WEIR

JOIN MY NEWSLETTER

CHAPTER ONE

aisy Barlow sneezed so loudly that it could almost be heard over the dreadful din of the machinery. Having spent half her young life working in the mill, it was a wonder that Daisy's nose was still made so sensitive by the tiny flying particles of cotton lint.

Janet, who was under one of the machines hastily tying the two ends of a snapped thread, slid out and stood upright, grinning like a fool and mimicking the motion of a sneeze before pretending to cover her ears against the sound.

Daisy laughed and shook her head. Her twin sister always made her laugh. However bad the day was, Janet Barlow could see some good in it, or if not the good, then at least a little humour. Daisy didn't know how other children managed the long days at the mill without a twin of their own to take the edge off things.

Daisy's attention was quickly returned to her work. Her mother, Vera, had seen her beloved girls out of the corner of her eye and quickly shook her head from side to side. Daisy knew her mother was just worried that Mr Baker would see and reprimand the girls or, worse still, dock their already meagre wages. And, of course, there was the ever-present threat of being reported to Mr Wainwright for misbehaving. He was famous for his short temper and penchant for the arbitrary dismissal of a mill worker without so much as a minute's hearing.

Turning to look at her mother, Daisy gave her a tiny nod to put her mind at rest and turned her eyes back to the loom. In return, Vera smiled at her daughter, so briefly that nobody could have accused her of not getting on with her work. Over the years, the family of three had developed their own system of silent communication in a world which was anything but.

Daisy turned her attention back to the shuttle quill she was loading with thread. She needed to be fast for Mr Baker didn't like the little things taking too much time. *Time was money*, that's what Mr Baker always said. Of course, for Daisy and her mother and sister, *time* was a *pittance*, for their pay barely kept them alive.

Daisy could see that Janet had already moved on from her amusement and was fully absorbed in wiping down. As far as Daisy could tell, it was just about the worst job in the entire mill. The worker, usually the younger children, would have to dart between the two heaviest parts of the power loom to wipe it down. In its practice, it wasn't any better or worse than many other jobs in the mill. To Daisy, however, the noise was horrendous. It was nothing compared to the inattentiveness of the man holding the carriage of the loom back on its brakes. Add in the sheer weight of the loom carriages —it made the whole thing more life-threatening.

Although she gave every appearance of working on her own task, Daisy watched the wiping down like a hawk when Janet was the child sent in to do it. She wanted to be ready to pull on the brakes herself if the man in charge of them let them go too quickly.

The problem was that Janet was small. They were

both thirteen years old, but Daisy was tall, and Janet was short and slight, like a tiny fairy. She was still able to take the same awful tasks that were reserved for children. At thirteen, Daisy and Janet were hardly that. No, children were five, six or at the most seven. At thirteen, childhood was long gone, if it had ever truly been there in the first place.

As she wound the thread back onto the shuttle, Daisy felt every nerve ending standing to attention. She moved a little to her right, closer to David Langley, the man standing at the brake lever. With her eyes darting back and forth between her sister and David, Daisy felt the dreadful sense of anxiety which seemed to sweep over her so many times in her working day. It was so common that it had come to feel like a perpetual state.

It was nearing the end of the day. A day which had begun sixteen hours before. It was the time of day, often referred to by the little ones as *the death time*. It was a disturbingly accurate description, for the last two hours of the working day were the hours in which most of the accidents happened. People who had worked for so many hours were exhausted enough, without the ceaseless noise of the machinery making it even harder to concentrate.

Shuttles banged from side to side, the engines roared, and the very walls of the mill seemed almost to shake. There was no escape from the din, and it was debilitating. All in all, *the death time* should have come as no surprise to anybody. Who could possibly concentrate as well in the *death time* as they had first thing in the morning after a little rest and a little quiet?

When Janet slid out from beneath the mule of the machine, Daisy breathed a sigh of relief. David let go of the brakes immediately, as he always did. Janet was barely clear of the loom when the carriage slid back with a bang loud enough to compete with so many other dreadful sounds. Langley always let go of the brakes like that. It was ingrained into them all that the machines should not be idle for long. When the machines stopped, the pay stopped. David Langley was in no better position than the Barlow family, and she could understand a poor man's desire to get the machine going straight away. Perhaps, he might have been a little less hasty had the person doing the wiping down been his own daughter or sister.

With her nerves shredded, Daisy knew that the final

hour of the working day couldn't pass by fast enough. She needed to be out of the noise and out of danger, letting go of the fear for a few hours until morning rolled around once more.

Janet was chattering to her as the girls and their mother got ready for the short journey home. It was a relief to get a little cool air, having suffered the tremendous heat of the mill for so many hours.

"I thought today would never end!" Janet said brightly, shouting instead of speaking, as so many mill workers did as they readjusted to the world outside of the unspeakable noise.

"Me too. I've almost sneezed my brains clean out today." Daisy was always ready to join in a little banter and have her beloved twin raise her spirits on the way home.

"Almost?" Janet was still loud, still adjusting. "They came right out, I saw them. They flew out of your nose and landed in Mr Baker's deep pockets!"

"Janet!" their mother hissed, looking over her shoulder.

"He's not here, is he, Mama? He's not out here with us of the bare-foot brigade searching for the right clogs to walk home in." Janet was giggling.

"Maybe he isn't here, my love, but there are them as would run to him and tell him if they thought it would do them some benefit. How many times do I have to tell you to take me seriously?" She lowered her voice. "And think of Mr Wainwright! He's as like to throw out an entire family as throw out just one noisy girl, isn't he? Then where shall we be?"

"Sorry, Mama," Janet was quiet now, her pretty face full of heartfelt apology as she eased her bare feet into her clogs.

Daisy smiled, Janet was the light of her life, but she knew their mother was right. They must always be careful when they spoke. Even at the end of the day when a myriad of workers, all of whom had worked barefoot in the mill room to avoid sparks from their clog irons igniting the snow-like cotton dust which covered the floors, were re-shooing themselves for the walk home.

Daisy wrapped her shawl around her tightly, making her way to the open door of the mill and out into the cool evening air. Working in the almost crippling heat and stifled recirculated air of the mill was almost like working in another country. The outside air always felt like something of a shock at the end of the working day, even if it was a blessed relief to draw a breath which didn't fill the lungs with soft cotton dust.

"What shall we have for our tea tonight?" Janet asked, chattering happily as they walked home, their clogs tapping a rhythmic beat as they went. "Shall we have venison?" she went on, laughing and completely recovered from their mother's telling-off.

"Or shall we have salmon and trout?" Daisy played along, always feeling a burst of relief at this time every day that the three of them had made it out of the mill for another day alive and with their full complement of fingers.

"Or shall we keep a hold of the real world and just eat the potato and cabbage stew we've been heating and re-heating all week long?" Vera stated with a sigh. She did, however, look at her girls and smile.

"Aye, let's do that! You can't beat cabbage at the end of a long day." Janet was as high-spirited at night as she was first thing in the morning.

"You've a fair humour on you, child, I'll give you that, but you tire me right enough," Vera said and laughed.

"Just think, in three days it will be Sunday. Nothing to do but go to church. No sounds but the birdsong to replace the looms." Daisy was getting in the spirit of things.

"Not you and all, Daisy!" Vera said and chuckled. "Not my sensible child! We've cleaning to be doing on Sunday as you very well know. That shameless charlatan of a landlord will be poking his beak into things, looking for some excuse to put the rent up again. No, my girl, we'll need to have the floor scrubbed and the mattresses tidied away in their corners. As the saying goes, there's no rest for the wicked."

"Then we must truly be the most wicked three females on earth, Mama, for there really is never a moment of rest," Daisy said and began to feel deflated.

"That won't help, my little chicken. Try to stay above it all like your sister does. It won't do to dwell."

It won't do to dwell was a phrase their mother had used day in, day out since their father had left them six years before when the twins were just seven. Vera had been right, of course, it really didn't do to dwell. There wasn't time to dwell, not even for the tiny girls who had been forced to work in the mill alongside their mother just to make ends meet.

Perhaps if their father had stayed, Janet wouldn't have to crawl between the loom carriage and the roller beam every day. Perhaps Daisy wouldn't have to swallow down the ball of fear in her throat each time. But Tom Barlow had gone, and he wasn't coming back. He'd left Burnley with his lover and had moved to goodness-knew-where to live in sin with her. Perhaps they had moved far enough away that they might pretend to be man and wife. Either way, Daisy Barlow would never, ever forgive him.

"Don't you think it's funny that Mr Baker is called Mr Baker, but he's not a baker, he works in a mill?" Janet said, clearly paying no heed to the more sensible conversation. "And that Mr Wainwright is called Mr Wainwright, but he isn't a wainwright, but the man who owns the mill. I suppose a relation of his must have been a wainwright at some time, don't you think, Mama?"

"I think you need to do less thinking, lass, if that's the best you can come up with!" Vera said, and they all laughed. "Come on, girls, let's get home!"

CHAPTER TWO

"*H*ave you not swept that lot up yet, Janet?" Vera Barlow asked with mild exasperation.

"Mama, I swept it up twice already. I don't know where it all comes from. That ceiling has been peeling for so long now that it's a wonder we're not just looking up at the clear sky!"

"Come on, Janet, let me sweep for a while," Daisy said and smiled at her sister as she took the broom. "She's right though, Mama, I remember this ceiling being in a dreadful state when we first came here after Father... well... when we first came here."

"Six years of peeling, day in, day out. It must be a

12

miracle of some kind that it hasn't peeled itself completely away." Janet sat on an upturned bucket in the middle of the room, the bucket she was to fill with water from the pump outside to wash the bare wooden floorboards of their one-room home in the Burnley slums.

"It'd be a bigger miracle if Joe Hamill had the place painted just once. And the wooden window frames are so rotten that as much cold air flies through this room when the windows are closed as when they are open. He really *is* a shameless charlatan, Mama," Daisy said, already having half the room swept.

"Be that as it may, there isn't a right lot we can do about it, Daisy. I don't know what sort of places you think the three of us can afford on our money." Sometimes Vera was just down, struggling beneath the weight of so much responsibility and hopelessness. "This is as good as our sort get."

"Mama, I know you don't mean that. It might be all we get, but it's not what we deserve. Joe Hamill might have clawed his way to own a rundown building or two, but he soon forgot where he came from, didn't he? He soon learned, like them rich ones do, that the best way of making money is either out of our pockets or off our backs. If the ceiling is peeling away to nothing, Mama, it's Joe Hamill's shame, not ours." Still sweeping, Daisy turned to look over her shoulder and smile at her mother. "The three of us do everything we can in this life, don't we?"

"That we do, my little chicken. That we do," Vera said and smiled back, making Daisy feel relieved.

By the time the Barlow family had paid their rent every week, there was very little left for anything else. The slums were the cheapest possible rent, but that rent was still far too high for what they received. It was a trap that the working poor fell into. A trap set by those who knew their circumstances well and had already discovered the best ways to profit by those circumstances. To keep a roof over their head, a poor family had nowhere else to go but the slums. That being the case, the landlord was free to allow the housing to fall into any state of disrepair he chose. Always reminding his tenants that if they were not happy, they might leave at any time. Always knowing that they couldn't afford to be anywhere better.

Daisy wasn't a vengeful girl, but she certainly spent a good part of her day hoping that the people who had

done the worst in this life, taken advantage of
made money from their plight, would suffer for
day as she and her kind had suffered. And it *was*
suffering to live in such a place, especially for a girl
who could remember what life was like before her
father had disappeared.

They'd never been wealthy, far from it, but they'd
rented a tiny two up two down terraced house in a
slightly cleaner part of Burnley. Knowing how to
read and write, Tom Barlow had occasionally found
himself in jobs which paid a little better than the
rest. It certainly wasn't enough for luxuries, but at
least his wife and daughters had a little more by way
of clothing than one dress for the week and one for
Sundays. When he had still been at home, they'd all
had a bonnet. However, years of wear and growing
had seen them all bonnet-less for some time now.

Their room was on the ground floor of a two-story
brick-built house. The walls had creeping mould
where the damp from the outside made its way
through the gaps and rotten woodwork after years of
neglect. Even though it never seemed to go
anywhere, Daisy spent a good part of every Sunday
with a brush and a pail of hot water trying to get rid
of it.

There was a fireplace in the room, over which the family cooked their meagre meals. There was a rail affixed to the chimney breast which held the family's only two pans and one spoon for stirring. There was an iron rail, which ended in a flat plate, set inside the fireplace, somewhere to set down a pan for cooking.

Their beds were no better than narrow mattresses on the floor, mattresses they'd had so long that Daisy couldn't even remember how and where they had acquired them, she only knew that they had never been brand-new to the family. No doubt countless people had slept on them before they'd made their way into the Barlow family's small abode.

They left the mattresses on the floor all week long, made up ready for them to crawl into after a long day's work. However, on Sundays, the mattresses were heaved up on their end, leaned against a wall, and covered with a sheet. Sunday was a day when Joe Hamill might appear at any moment, and Vera not only wanted to avoid him declaring the place to be a mess and adding a shilling to the rent, but she had her own pride too. Their home might not have been much, but she was determined to keep it clean and decent.

In fact, Vera was so determined that there was only a pot to be used in emergencies. Otherwise, she and her daughters wandered out of the back of the house, day or night, to the shared privy at the far end of the row. Daisy hated the shared privy. Nobody ever seemed to take responsibility for keeping it clean, and as a result, it was an awful place.

"Have you not swept that lot up yet, Daisy?" Janet asked, parroting her mother's earlier words and grinning like a court jester.

"I never knew anybody as cheeky as you!" Daisy said, trying to sound stern but unable to keep her amusement out of her voice, much less her face.

"What would life be like if I wasn't around to be cheeky anymore? Dull, that's what!" Janet said and got to her feet, picking up the bucket she'd been sitting on and heading out of the door to fill it at the pump.

As Daisy swept up the last curls of peeled paint, she looked over at her mother. They smiled at one another; they knew that life was made better by Janet and her cheeky ways.

It was late on Wednesday, and Daisy could hardly believe that they still had three full sixteen-hour days of work to do before Sunday came around again. Why was it that Sunday passed by so quickly and the rest of the week dragged along in noise and dust and worry?

"Daisy," Mr Baker had come up beside her and bellowed in her ear, trying to make himself heard over the machinery. "Go across to the back loom, the thread keeps snapping. I know your hands aren't tiny, but you're nimble enough. But mind you concentrate; I don't want to have to shut off the machine if you lose a finger in there."

Daisy stared at him for a moment before a gentle shove propelled her in the right direction. She didn't want to be on the other side of the mill, she always liked to have her mother and sister close enough to see. However, Mr Baker, the man who managed the day-to-day running of the mill for Mr Wainwright, was not a man to be argued with. So, Daisy hurried through the room, her bare feet kicking up the soft, fluffy cotton dust as she went.

The other loom really did need looking at and looking at properly. The thread was snapping every few minutes, and there was clearly either a problem with the bobbins or the gap settings on the loom itself. Either way, if she simply kept re-tying the threads, somebody would later be complaining about having to trim the loose ones off the fabric, possibly even Mr Baker himself.

After almost half an hour of tying the threads, the decision was made to shut down the loom and fix the problem. Daisy could see the disappointment on so many faces, none of them keen to take the drop in pay that inevitably resulted from one of the looms going down, whether it was their fault or not.

It was time for Daisy to get out of the way and Mr Baker, without words, pointed her back across to her original work of making sure that the shuttles flew through the threads easily on each pass. Her mother was doing the same job a few feet away from her, her focus fully absorbed. As Daisy resumed her own work, she scanned the room for any sign of Janet.

Not seeing her anywhere, she felt that little sense of panic she always felt. This time, however, there was a sudden prickling at the back of her neck, a sense of dreadful foreboding. Taking her eyes off her own work entirely, Daisy realised that one of the looms had been opened, its carriage drawn out and held back on brakes. No doubt Janet, small and nimble, was inside, crouched down, wiping away the dust which choked the looms so regularly.

As always, Daisy fixed her attention on David Langley. She could see that the man regularly looked over his shoulder at the unfolding drama of the dormant loom at the back of the room. With his hand on the brake lever, Daisy held her breath. Why couldn't the man just concentrate on what he was doing, instead of worrying what the closed loom was going to do to his pay packet?

With the greatest sense that something was about to go wrong, Daisy felt a horrible feeling in the pit of her stomach. Even though nothing had yet happened, she had a sense that it was already too late. Daisy left her post and began to cross to where David was. She crouched down as she made her way, looking for any sign of Janet and seeing her similarly crouched just exactly where she expected to see her; between the carriage and the roller beam.

As if it was always going to happen, the distracted

David Langley, likely as bone-tired as the rest of them and in need of a break, absentmindedly pushed at the brake lever. Daisy opened her mouth to scream, her arms spread wide as she tried to get the man's attention. However, her scream died in the noise of the room, and she knew that it was already too late the moment he had pushed the brake lever.

The carriage flew back instantly, that horrible bang as it settled into place once more. Daisy dropped to the floor, scrabbling on her hands and knees, trying to find her sister. Perhaps the only saving grace, when she did find her, was to know that it would have been quick. Janet wouldn't have lingered.

Crushed between the back of the loom carriage and the immovable roller beam, Janet Barlow's head lolled to one side, her chest and shoulders flattened. The heavy machinery pinned her there in such a position, such a garish, awful position, that Daisy knew she would never forget it for the rest of her life.

Daisy, on her hands and knees, was violently sick. Bit by bit, the room began to fall silent. There was a commotion behind her, all around her the men were powering down the looms. Bare feet were running backwards and forwards in a blind panic. It was the first time in the six years that Daisy had worked in the mill that the machines had all been powered down at once, and it seemed that the sudden silence caused a great pressure inside her ears, inside her head.

Suddenly realising that there was somebody at her side, Daisy tried to turn to look, but couldn't take her eyes off her sister. Her beloved twin sister; the other half of her. The funny half, the light-hearted half, the tiny and most precious half.

It was only when she heard her mother's heartbroken screams that she realised that it was *she* crouched down by her side, *she* who was staring across at the broken, lifeless body of the daughter she couldn't reach.

CHAPTER THREE

"*M*ama, it's nearly time," Daisy said the following afternoon. She could hear the barrow man outside, the wheels of his barrow unmistakable on the cobbles.

Daisy could hear him calling to his lad, the young boy who always ran along at the side of the long barrow, telling him to help him down with the box. Daisy felt sick; it *was* a box, for nobody seeing it could ever truly describe it as a coffin.

Coffins, real coffins, were buried in the earth along with their occupants, not used simply to hide a body from public view before it was tipped out into an open paupers' grave and loaded back up onto the barrow ready to house the next poor unfortunate to let go their hold on life.

"No, no," Vera said, on her knees on the bare floor beside the mattress upon which Janet's ruined body had been laid the evening before. "Janet's not ready to go yet, she isn't. She said she's not ready to go, Daisy, and I won't make her."

"Mama, please," Daisy said, tears streaming down her face. "She's not here, she's gone," her voice was a whisper, but even if it had been a shout, Daisy knew it wouldn't have got through. It wouldn't have permeated this strange consciousness her mother now seemed to inhabit.

She hurried across the room and outside, coming face-to-face with the barrow man. He was carrying the box, with the help of his lad, and he looked at Daisy with kindness.

"I don't know what to do, Mr Sharp. My mama has been hanging over my sister's body all night and all morning, never once letting go of her. I don't think she'll let her go, even though she must, and I don't know what to do."

"It'll be hard for her, right enough," Mr Sharp said

and turned to look at his lad, motioning to him with a nod. They set the box down on the cobbles. "I was shocked to hear it, myself. That little Janet was always so lively, always a smile on that pretty face of hers. Them there mills are evil places, my girl, and I thank God Almighty himself every night that I have this little barrow of mine to make a living. Poor Janet; poor little scrap," he said and shook his head, looking emotional.

Daisy knew that Mr Sharp had seen his fair share of death and destruction in his time collecting the bodies of those who had lived and died in the slums. Bodies which he transported and dumped, often from a great height, on top of the bodies of those who had gone before. It was the sort of living that a person had to harden themselves to, no doubt about it, but the fact that he seemed to have been so affected by the gruesome and untimely death of Janet Barlow made Daisy's loss all the more real. Everyone had loved Janet; everyone.

Well, everybody except Mr Wainwright, apparently, who had given Janet's mother and sister just one day to have the dead girl buried, and their grieving done, before returning to work. Daisy couldn't think of it, the awfulness of it all. Janet killed on Wednesday afternoon, her mother and sister returning to work on the Friday morning. That wasn't the passing of a life observed, it was simply an inconvenience, like one of the machines being shut down.

"Your mother's had an awful shock, Daisy. You both have, and I couldn't be sorrier for it. There's no relief in me making my living today, and that's the truth. It's getting late though, my sweet, and if we don't get Janet to the grave soon, the reverend will have gone for the day, and there'll be nobody to say a few words for her. You know, one of God's representatives here on earth, so to speak." He nodded respectfully and stooped down to pick up the box again, his lad silently followed suit.

Daisy went ahead of Mr Sharp into the house, knowing that she would have to find some way to prise her mother away from Janet for the last time.

It was every bit as awful as Daisy had imagined and more besides. Vera seemed to have let go of her senses, trying to climb onto the mattress beside her dead daughter, scowling at Daisy and accusing her of trying to steal her away. It was almost as if her mother didn't know who she was anymore. As if she didn't recognise her.

In the end, Mr Sharp himself had been forced to take hold of Vera, and he pulled her away, leaving Daisy to hold tightly to her whilst he and his lad hurriedly put Janet's body into the box. They wasted no time in rushing outside with her, putting the box onto the barrow, and getting ready to walk away.

"Come on, Mama. We have to walk down there with her, we can't let her be put into the ground alone," Daisy said, her heart so broken that her chest ached. Her mother had slid to the floor, like a life-sized ragdoll, unable to move her limbs, unable to function.

It had taken every ounce of strength Daisy had to get her mother to her feet, but it was no good. As soon as she had her mother upright, she simply dropped to the floor again, landing hard like a stone. Hearing the wheels of the barrow on the cobbles slowly rolling away, Daisy knew she had to do something. Her mother wasn't up to this, she wasn't able, and Janet was already making her final journey alone.

Having to leave her mother there on the floor, Daisy ran out into the street, catching up with the barrow man, catching up with Janet. This would be the last journey the twins would ever make together, and

Daisy didn't know how she was going to live her life without the other half of herself.

The following morning, after another night without a moment of sleep, Daisy boiled some water over the fire and made her and her mother some hot tea. Tea leaves weren't a thing that the Barlow family often laid out the money for, but one of their neighbours had given Daisy a small brown paper bag of them, enough to make four pots of tea if she made it weak enough.

"Here, Mama, drink this. And eat this, you'll need your strength today," Janet said as she handed her mother a hard wedge of bread, days old and already stale. With everything that had happened, Daisy hadn't had the wherewithal to bake her and her mother something fresh, not even a little flour and water flatbread on the iron plate over the fire.

"Thank you, Janet," Vera said, smiling up at Daisy, clearly not seeing her for who she really was. "You're a good girl, even if you *are* cheeky. I don't know what I'd do without you and your fooling from morning till night, really, I don't. I don't know what Daisy would do without you either." She sat holding the handle of the tin mug, steam rising in front of her face unobserved.

Vera was still sitting on the floor where she'd sat all night, where she'd been ever since Janet's body had been taken from the room. She peered down at the bread in her hand for a moment, as if wondering how on earth it had got there. She let go of it, and it sat there on her lap, hard and dry.

"Mama, you know we only have a few minutes longer before we have to leave for the day?" Daisy said, feeling horribly alone in the world.

"Of course, I do, cheeky!" Vera said and started to laugh. "I know when it's time to leave for the mill, Janet, don't I?" It was as if nothing had ever happened, as if she had no idea whatsoever that Janet's body lay on top of so many others in the pauper's grave, a shovel full of lime on top of her keeping the miasma at bay until the grave was full and finally covered with soil.

"Of course, you do, Mama," Daisy said, playing along even as her heart ached. She was still in shock herself, her mind so full of awful images that she barely dared to close her eyes, and yet she knew she must keep going. She was in this alone for as long as her mother denied reality. "But you do need to eat, Mama. Come on, get that bread down you." She spoke cheerfully, trying to cajole her.

When her mother simply sat smiling at her, Daisy knelt on the floor beside her, plucking the piece of dry bread from her lap and handing it to her. When Vera made no move to eat, Daisy gently took hold of her wrist and elbow and levered her arm up until the bread rested against her dry lips. Finally, Vera Barlow took a bite, chewed it, and swallowed. She raised the mug of tea and chased the rough bread down her throat with a deep gulp.

If nothing else, this was a start. But how was her mother going to react to the mill? How was she going to stand in the very spot she had stood on when her thirteen-year-old daughter had been crushed to death? Surely, the memory would come back, surely the denial of it all would be futile then.

"We haven't got time to sit here sipping tea, my sweet," Vera said when she'd hurriedly finished the meagre meal and began to get to her feet. She brushed down the front of her dress as she so often did, stood up straight, and pressed her hands to the back of her head to be sure that her tight bun was in position. That there were no loose hairs which might see her caught in the machinery, her scalp lifted from her head as so many had suffered before.

In almost every respect, her mother seemed normal. It was as if she had suddenly sprung to life, getting herself ready for the day ahead as if this day was just like any other day. She even hummed to herself, the pretty little tune she so often hummed. Daisy's throat was tight with emotion, with fear, and she fought hard not to cry. She needed to get her mother to work, she needed to have them both there earning their money, or Mr Wainwright would turn them out. If it meant letting her mother hold onto her pretence, then that's exactly what Daisy would have to do.

"Come on then, Janet!" Vera said, with a broad smile as she stared right at Daisy. "If we don't get a move on, we won't catch Daisy up. Goodness, she must be there already." She hurried to the door, took her heavy shawl down from the hook, and wrapped it around her shoulders.

Daisy followed suit, smiling at her mother, battling

with the emotions which were coursing through her body like blood. The two of them walked along the street, their clog irons clicking as they went.

"As I said, she must already be there. But it's early, isn't it?" Vera said and turned to look at Daisy. "She did leave, didn't she? Oh, she's a sensible girl, she'll be ahead of us. But where is she? I can't see her," she was talking fast, staring right into Daisy's eyes. "Where on earth is Daisy?" She shrugged her shoulders and hurried on, leaving Daisy to clip along behind her.

"I'm right here, Mama. I'm right here," Daisy said, tears streaming down her face at last.

CHAPTER FOUR

*V*era Barlow remained the same for days on end. She talked as if her daughter was still alive, always wondering where it was that Daisy had got to. Daisy was on tenterhooks the whole time, watching her mother like a hawk at work, finally grateful for the pervasive noise which had stopped anyone around hearing her speak or giving herself away. It was something of a mystery to Daisy how her mother managed to do her work, remembering every process even if she couldn't remember how her daughter had died right there just a week before.

For her own part, Daisy was so vigilant, her senses heightened as she watched for any signs of a sudden deterioration in her mother's condition. David Langley was there, his face ashen, dark circles around his eyes telling of as many nights without sleep as Daisy had suffered. Daisy tried to imagine how she would feel if she'd been the cause of another's death, but she could only sustain an altruistic heart for a matter of minutes at a time. For the rest of the time, she simply couldn't look at David.

Daisy knew that the real cause of Janet's death was a mixture of punishingly long hours, the dreadful noise, and the panic in the hearts of all the mill workers when one of the looms was powered down. David had been distracted, looking over his shoulder to the loom that was out of action. His sense of panic was real, as was the panic of them all. Most were just managing to survive, and even a shilling less in their pay often meant the difference between eating and paying the full week's rent. It was the likes of Mr Wainwright devising such cruel rules, and the likes of Mr Baker stridently enforcing them, that was really to blame. David had just been the man with his hand on the brake lever.

It wasn't until the loom Vera was working on needed wiping down that the unreality of her world was finally broken. The loom had been wiped down many times, but Vera had seemed to hardly notice. Why she broke when she did was a mystery to Daisy, but when she broke, she broke into tiny pieces.

The carriage of the loom had been pulled forward along its rails and the brakes applied by David. Daisy could see how the poor man's attention was on the child beneath the mule the entire time. The concentration on his face, the tremor in his arms, was as if his own life depended on it. Daisy watched him like a hawk, her stomach churning just as it always did, even though Janet was no longer there to perform the task.

When the child was free from the machine, standing some feet from its side, David stood almost paralysed with his hand over the lever. Daisy could see him shaking before he crouched down to look beneath the loom to be absolutely certain that there was nobody there. Something about his action drew Vera's attention, and she paused in her own work for a moment, her head tilted to one side as she studied him with interest.

Finally, he pulled at the brake lever, releasing the carriage and watching it fly back across the rails, landing back into position with its customary bang. It was at that moment that, even over the dreadful din inside the mill room, Daisy heard her mother's bloodcurdling scream.

Daisy immediately began to shake as her mother dropped to the floor, scrabbling on all fours up and down the full length of the loom, roaring for her child, searching for her as she went. Daisy darted over to her, trying to put her arms around her, but Vera was just too quick for her and just too determined.

She was screaming at David to draw back the carriage, to free the child that wasn't even there. Despite Daisy's best efforts, Vera would not calm down, and with so much noise in the room, she couldn't listen to Daisy's reasoning. Finally, not only was the spectacle drawing the attention of all around, but it had caught the eye of Mr Baker.

He marched over, his countenance cold and uncaring, his brow furrowed in anger because of the distraction caused to the rest of the mill workers. He was shouting, Daisy could tell that much at least, although she wasn't entirely sure what he was saying. In the end, to make his point absolutely clear, he roughly took hold of Vera's shoulders and dragged her to her feet, trying to pull her away from the loom.

However, Vera fought him ferociously, so sure that Janet was still there. Still afraid that her girl was trapped between the loom carriage and the roller beam, her upper torso crushed beyond recognition, her heart and lungs flattened and useless to her. With a strength that Daisy had never realised her mother possessed, she began to push Mr Baker, screaming into his face, shaking him as he had shaken her.

They were moving ever closer to the working loom, and Mr Baker, his back to the machinery, was now at the sort of risk that the workers suffered day in, day out. In the end, he was forced to break free from Vera, and Daisy tried to take hold of her mother, to hold her, to calm her. However, Vera was still struggling, still trying to crawl beneath the working loom, desperate to rescue the child who was already dead and buried.

Finally, all the looms were powered down, and the room fell silent, barring the demented screams of Vera Barlow. Mr Baker, furious at having been attacked, despite his own unnecessary harshness towards a broken woman, ordered two of the largest male mill workers to seize Vera, to hold onto her tightly until policemen could be called.

When two policemen finally arrived, more than twenty minutes later, Vera was still screaming out her pain, letting go of her senses altogether as she continued to fight like a wildcat. As her mother was dragged away, taken into police custody, nobody would listen to Daisy. She was trying to tell the policemen that her sister had been killed right in front of their mother just a week before, but they were in no mood to listen. What did they care for a woman's pain? *A mother's pain.* And Mr Baker, that vile man, was so determined to see his version of justice done that there was no way the policemen could have left the mill that day without their prisoner.

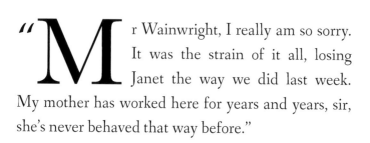

"Mr Wainwright, I really am so sorry. It was the strain of it all, losing Janet the way we did last week. My mother has worked here for years and years, sir, she's never behaved that way before."

"I cannot have one of my supervisors almost murdered by a deranged woman, child. And those looms have been powered down for more than half an hour today, do you have any idea how much money you and your mother have cost me?"

"Mr Wainwright, do you have any idea what it cost us to see my sister crushed to death inside one of your looms? My mother wasn't given time to recover, just one day to bury her daughter, and straight back to work. I asked Mr Baker for a little more time, but he told me that if we did not come in, we needn't bother coming back again. Can you not see how cruel that is? Can you not see how a mother might break in two under such stress and without a moment to grieve?" Daisy was sobbing, terrified for what would happen to her mother, and terrified for what would happen to her. She had never spoken to Mr Wainwright before, and he was the most intimidating man.

He was tall and broad, his greying hair grisly, his mutton chop sideburns full. His eyes were pale blue but fierce, and he studied Daisy as if she were no better than a specimen on a glass slide beneath a microscope.

"I do not run a charity, child. It is enough that I give you people work without having to put up with your day-to-day needs. Now, it is regrettable that your sister died, I am not a hard-hearted man by any means, but likely she did not behave as instructed; young girls are apt to be distracted. As difficult as it is, there is nobody to blame for your sister's death but your sister herself. Perhaps it would have been better if your mother had raised her to concentrate. Perhaps that is why your mother has reacted so violently today... she sees her own part in all of this, and the guilt is too much for her. Yes, that will be it. That will be it, all right." He nodded as if pleased to have come up with the sort of reasoning which would release him from any responsibility.

Of course, there was nobody for Mr Wainwright to answer to in the case of Janet's death. Despite the government's pretence of caring an ounce for the lives of the country's workers, they had still only engaged just four factory inspectors to cover the entire country. It was little wonder that the mill in Burnley had never once seen an inspector. That none of these inspectors had ever witnessed the machinery still running as children picked fluff and lost fingers, the law flouted with nobody to see, nobody to complain to.

"Sir, I am begging for your mercy in my mother's case. I'm sure that you can see that it was the pain of losing a child which broke her. She doesn't deserve to be prosecuted, to go to prison for it. Please, Mr Wainwright, won't you speak out in her defence?"

"To speak out in her defence, child, would be to suggest that I am somehow to blame for your sister's death, would it not?" Although he spoke with the same northern accent that she did, it was a little clipped in its attempt at refinement and delivered with such confidence that it was no more than arrogance.

"I don't think so, sir. If you could just..."

"No, you do not get to direct me, child. You forget who pays your wages, it would appear. Now then, as far as I can see, it has been more than an hour and a half since you have produced work of any kind. On this occasion, I will not dock it from your wages, but if you do not return to your loom immediately, then I will have no choice but to dismiss you. I cannot encourage this sort of thing in my workers, and if I am lenient with one, I will be expected to be lenient with the rest, and then where will I be? The workhouse, that's where!"

Daisy could hardly believe what she was hearing; the man really could only spare a thought for himself.

Without a word, Daisy turned away from him and walked out of his office. She walked back into the mill room, knowing that eyes flicked to her from all around, some of them with sympathy, some of them furious that the looms had been powered down and it would likely be reflected in their own wages.

Poverty made people hard, it took their souls. It stopped them standing shoulder to shoulder, supporting one another, denying the rich the right to treat them this way. That was how the likes of Mr Wainwright survived, thrived, made themselves fat and rich on the broken bodies of the poor who would, as long as they stood alone and not together, never, ever complain.

Almost mechanically, Daisy set to work once more. Tears rolled down her face as she thought of her mother, wondering what was happening to her now, wondering what would happen to her in the future.

Would she be allowed to return to the mill afterwards? If not, how were they to manage? Would her reason return? Would she ever be able to function again in a normal manner?

It occurred to Daisy that, just a matter of days before, none of this was a concern. Janet was alive, smiling and laughing, keeping them going. How could everything change so suddenly? How could their lives be destroyed so completely? Images came at her one by one as if trying to finish her too. Her sister crushed, the look of pain in her dead eyes so appalling. Her broken body thrown on top of so many others in the open pauper's grave, a shovel full of lime thrown down on top of her to spare the living the dreadful odour of the dead. And now her mother, dragged away by two policemen, likely to be charged at the behest of the very men who had, by their cruelty and appalling conditions, caused the whole thing in the first place.

There was nothing she could do but carry on. There was nothing she could do but carefully reach into the loom and free the shuttle that had become trapped.

There was nothing she could do.

CHAPTER FIVE

Daisy shook as she approached the asylum in Lancaster. It had taken some time to walk from the train station to the building itself, and she was tired and thirsty. She hadn't seen her mother since the day she had lost her reason in the mill, and she had cried every night with loneliness. How could she be so alone when, just weeks before, she'd had a mother and a sister at home with her?

The building looked appalling, such an imposing, frightening sight. It was built in the gothic style, with a central clock tower and two long wings in which the inmates were housed. She was met by a rough-looking man at the gate, who finally let her through when she explained that she had come to visit her mother. Daisy was most determined; most of her Sunday would be spent travelling, and she certainly wasn't going to leave without setting eyes on her beloved mother.

She walked along a wide pathway, lawns and pretty gardens either side of her, a strange addition to a place that looked otherwise so without hope.

"My name is Daisy Barlow, and I've come to see my mother, Vera Barlow," Daisy said to a very austere looking nurse who stepped out in front of her the moment she entered the building.

"You will have to wait here, you can't simply walk in and expect to be accommodated," the nurse said, scowling at her. The woman was tall, heavyset although she was lean, with jet black hair pulled sharply away from her face, a small and neat white cap over the top of it. She wore a dark grey dress, high-necked and long-sleeved, with an immaculate white apron over the top.

"I have come all the way from Burnley, Miss," Daisy said, hoping to appeal to the woman's sense of decency.

"I am not *Miss*; I am *Sister* Ryan!" the nurse went on, most affronted.

"Forgive me," Daisy said and tried to smile.

"I will speak to Dr Winchester; he is in charge of your mother's case. Wait here, as I said, and do not go wandering."

Before Daisy had a chance to respond, the nurse walked smartly away.

Left alone in the entrance, Daisy felt afraid. The asylum was noisy, although not nearly as noisy as the mill room was. However, the sounds were so much more disturbing, being wails and groans and cries, screams and shouts. It was a place of great distress, and Daisy could feel it seeping in through the pores of her skin, filling her with even more hopelessness than sat inside her already.

She looked down a long corridor, a corridor which was jointed along its length by great stone arches. It reminded her a little of church if church had been a place for troubled minds in the deepest despair.

"Follow me!" Sister Ryan had returned, still scowling, still disapproving.

Daisy said nothing, she simply followed along in the nurse's wake, her nerves already jangling terribly as she wondered what she was about to be confronted with. She couldn't bear the idea of her mother being in this place, these high stone walls and despair. But she couldn't bear the idea of setting eyes on her to find that no improvement had come, or even that she had grown worse, more demented. To find that her stay in such a place was doing more harm than good.

However, she was taken to the doctor's office, the nurse knocking abruptly on the door before opening it and rather roughly pushing Daisy inside as if she herself were an inmate.

"Barlow's daughter," Sister Ryan said by way of introduction. "This is Dr Winchester, and you would do well to mind your manners."

It occurred to Daisy that the nurse was speaking to her as if she were an employee, just as Mr Baker might speak to her back at the mill. It made her angry, and Daisy, finding her courage, glared back at the woman. Her glare hit its mark, for it caught the heartless nurse off guard and it showed in her look of surprise.

"Ah good, *Mrs* Barlow's daughter," the doctor said, emphasising Vera Barlow's title, something which struck Daisy as rather pointed; did he, too, disapprove of Sister Ryan's harshness?

"I'm Daisy Barlow, Dr Winchester," Daisy said, politely introducing herself.

"You will speak when you're spoken to," Sister Ryan said, but Daisy did not respond.

"That will be all, thank you, Sister," Dr Winchester said, and Daisy was certain that she could hear the faintest tone of annoyance in his cultured voice. With a huff of disapproval, the nurse walked out of the room and closed the door behind her.

"Please take a seat, Miss Barlow," Dr Winchester said, and smiled at her, a kindly smile which felt to Daisy like the first act of kindness she had enjoyed since her sister had been killed. Certainly, nobody at the mill had troubled much about her, most of them still blaming her for the dock in pay they had suffered.

"Thank you, Doctor. I haven't seen my mother since she... *collapsed*," she said, not knowing how to put it.

"She was taken away before I had a chance to do or say anything in her favour."

"Perhaps you would be able to tell me a little something of it all, Miss Barlow. I'm afraid I was given no information barring the fact that your mother had attacked a manager in the mill, almost killing him as she tried to push him into a working loom," he said, his eyes narrowed as if he hadn't quite believed the story in the first place.

"And nothing more, sir?" Daisy asked, her eyes filling with tears at the injustice of it all. "Nothing from the police or the magistrate about how my mother had seen one of her daughters crushed to death just days before in that very room?"

"Oh, Miss Barlow, I am so very sorry," Dr Winchester said, and she could tell by the look in his eyes that he meant it.

He had a kindly face, a very pleasant, handsome face. He was perhaps thirty years of age, but he looked tired and somewhat careworn. He had dark brown hair, very dark indeed, but his bright blue eyes were the thing which gave him away as a man who was just a little younger than he might have appeared. He wore dark clothing; black trousers and a waistcoat, both sporting faint, widely spaced pinstripes. His shirt was brilliant white, the collars high and held in place by a black necktie. He wore no coat, but Daisy could see it hanging from the hat stand in the corner of the room. It was long, thigh length, with the same faint pinstriping of the rest of his suit. As it was, his pristine white sleeves were folded back to the elbow, giving every appearance of a man who engaged fully with his working life.

"A week before my mother broke, my twin sister, Janet, was crushed between the carriage and roller beam of one of the looms in the mill where we all worked in Burnley. My mother and I were witness to it all, and we were given one day free of work, unpaid of course, to have her buried."

"And did your mother lose her reason immediately?"

"No, Doctor," Daisy said, trying to hold back her tears as she remembered every stage of their loss. "She seemed to understand what was happening in the beginning, it was all so awful, so shocking. Janet was brought home on a cart, laid out on a mattress in the room we live in, to be collected the following day by the barrow man and taken to a pauper's grave." It wasn't for any lack of pride, but Daisy wanted this man to know exactly what it was like to suffer in her world. She wasn't going to hold back a single drop of the experience.

"And you both attended the funeral?"

"Funeral?" Daisy said and closed her eyes, trying to remember that this man had probably never experienced a day's genuine discomfort in his whole life. "There was no funeral, Dr Winchester. My sister was taken on a cart to an open grave and thrown in on top of everybody else who had died before her that week. The Reverend was supposed to be there to say a few words, but he had other pressing matters to attend to. So, my sister was thrown into the ground, her body covered with lime, and that was that."

"How did your mother react?"

"She didn't, she wasn't there. I had to leave her back at home, collapsed upon the floor. She was so distraught that the barrow man had to help me to pull her off my sister's body so that it could be loaded and taken away. I couldn't get her up from the floor, and I didn't have any choice but to leave her there. I didn't want my sister to be buried without... I mean..." She couldn't help it; she started to cry.

"I really am so very sorry to have you go through it all again, Miss Barlow," he said, taking a handkerchief from his own pocket and handing it to her across the desk. "I wish I didn't have to ask you, but with so few details from the authorities as to why they decided to commit your mother, I have nothing to work with, no path to follow in hopes of repairing her tortured mind."

"Do you think she can be repaired?"

"Grief and shock certainly affect people in different ways, Miss Barlow. Many of my patients here have what I would term *organic* mental collapses. There is something wrong with them, you see, something not caused by circumstance, and it is extraordinarily difficult to treat. Although I do not want to give you false hope, suffice it to say that, if your mother's breakdown was caused by an event external to her mind, there is a chance that she might be reached."

"It was the following morning that I truly realised she'd let go of her reason," Daisy sniffed and continued, determined to help her mother in any way she could. "She seemed to be back to normal at first, cheerful and even laughing, getting herself ready for work. It was unnerving to see, and more unnerving when she called me *Janet*. It was as if nothing had happened, as if my sister was still alive. She kept asking me where Daisy was as if I had just wandered out of the room."

"She had disassociated entirely from the event," the doctor said in a low voice, looking at some papers on his desk and nodding thoughtfully. "How long did that attitude persist?"

"For almost a week, sir. She had worked every day, carrying out her tasks just as normal. It is such a noisy place that the workers can't really speak to one another, and at the end of a sixteen-hour day, we are too tired to linger and share a conversation of any kind. So, I suppose we got away with it for a few days. That was until she watched the man who had accidentally let the brakes go with the loom when my sister was still inside. He was performing the same operation and I could see her watching him intently. When he let go of the brakes, even though it was safe to do so, my mother screamed. She screamed and tried to crawl under the loom, believing my sister to be there, I think. It was then that the supervisor, Mr

Baker, pulled her to her feet and began to shake her. She was determined to get back to the loom, she was trying to push him away, but he had his back to the loom, and that is why he claimed that she had tried to kill him. If he had left her, if he had not been so rough with her, it wouldn't have happened."

"Did she come to her senses at all?"

"No, she was held roughly by two of the other mill workers as she screamed and tried to free herself. Finally, the policemen came, and they dragged her away, still screaming for her daughter and trying to escape so that she might help her. That was the last I saw of her."

"She was committed by a magistrate, so she was obviously taken to the court to answer charges," he said, giving a great sigh and shaking his head. "And that, presumably, was when the magistrate saw fit to have her committed. You did not go to the proceedings?"

"No, I had no idea that one had been called. I attended the police station when I could, but it was always after I had finished my work at the mill, and there never seemed to be anybody there who would tell me what was happening. They didn't care, I suppose that's the truth of it."

"And you are still working at the mill?"

"I don't have any choice, Dr Winchester. I could only come here today because it's Sunday and I don't work on a Sunday. To take a moment away from the mill now will result in my dismissal. Mr Wainwright, the mill owner, has already told me as much."

"I see," the doctor said and shook his head from side to side as if he couldn't quite believe it.

"Is she any better? Is she any better at all?"

"No, not yet. Perhaps if you come along with me now to see her, there might be some change. Do you think you are ready?"

"Yes, of course," Daisy was already on her feet.

CHAPTER SIX

*D*aisy was taken to a room which resembled a prison cell. There were only women in that part of the asylum, but they were no less frightening as far as Daisy was concerned. Most were unkempt, some in old and dirty nightgowns, one or two of them chained to the wall by their ankles.

The chained ones seemed more disturbed than the rest, trying to free themselves, reaching out for others, yelling and spitting. Other women simply wandered up and down, up and down, taking five or six paces in one direction and then turning around to take five or six in the other, repeating the process over and over.

The walls of the room were high, and the windows several feet above them, wide arches of light lessening the gloom. There were at least fifteen women in the room, but the cries from other rooms told Daisy very clearly that there were other cells just like this, and she hardly dared imagine how many.

The appearance of Daisy and the doctor in the room had a great effect on the inhabitants, some of whom backed away, and some of whom made their way towards them. Dr Winchester spoke kindly, gently turning away those who came up to him. However, when two nurses came into the room, one of them Sister Ryan, *all* the women backed away. Daisy couldn't help but wonder how difficult it must be to be a kind man surrounded by people who were anything but.

"Mama!" Daisy said above the growing noise when she spotted her mother alone in the far corner of the room. She was sitting on the floor, her dress, the very dress she had worn that last day, filthy from top to bottom. She was staring blankly ahead of her, her knees drawn into her chest, her thin arms wrapped around those knees as she rocked gently backwards and forwards. Her hair, which was always neatly wound onto the back of her head in a bun, hung loose and long, seeming somehow much more wiry than normal, making her look a little witch-like.

"Sister Ryan, can you help Mrs Barlow up from the floor and take her to an empty room, we need a little quiet," Dr Winchester said firmly.

"Certainly, Dr Winchester," the nurse said, still smarting from his dismissal of her earlier.

Although she and the other nurse gently helped Vera to her feet, Daisy was certain that neither of those women would be so kind to her mother once the eyes of the doctor were elsewhere. Sister Ryan had a vindictive look, and there would be no doubt that she would take her anger out on one of the inmates later, most likely Daisy's mother.

The nurses led Vera away, with Dr Winchester and Daisy following in their wake. They were all taken into a room which had a table and some chairs, an old metal filing cabinet, and a fireplace which looked as if it hadn't been lit for years.

"Thank you, if you could wait outside," Dr Winchester said to the nurses.

"Mama, Mama, it's me. It's Daisy." Her mother had been settled into a chair but was still rocking. Daisy knelt in front of her, trying to take her hands, but her mother resisted, holding her hands up out of the way and refusing to look at Daisy.

It was more vague resistance than active. As if she had no idea that it was her own daughter there before her.

"She doesn't know me, does she?"

"I think she is so deeply disturbed by what happened to your sister that she doesn't know *anybody*. I don't believe that she knows where she is, or perhaps even *who* she is. As I said before, I don't want to give you false hope, but I shall keep working with her. Perhaps time and patience will help. If I can at least get her to talk, then perhaps I can get her to discuss the terrible trauma."

"But will that help? Won't reliving it all make her feel worse?"

"Miss Barlow, it has to come out. At the moment, it's trapped deep inside of her, and I suspect that her break with reality is her mind's way of protecting her from the truth. I cannot be certain, of course, but if I can find a way to have her face the truth, she might be able to grieve properly, to let the whole thing out. Without the truth, I do not believe there will be any reason."

"I just wish she could see me. I just wish she could know that I'm here." Daisy tentatively laid her hand on her mother's leg, so gently that her mother didn't even notice. She just wanted that touch, to have human contact with her last remaining family member. Having just that much, Daisy wanted more. It was an effort not to throw her arms around her mother and cling to her, begging her to come back to her senses and help her only daughter through this nightmare. But she didn't, she stayed calm.

"Miss Barlow, I really will do everything I can to help her. Perhaps if you could come every week?" he said, and she knew it was a question. He was asking after her circumstances, tentatively trying to find out if it was possible.

"I will try very hard, Dr Winchester, but with only my wage coming in now, I don't really know how I'm going to manage. The added expense of the journey might be too much." Again, tears rolled down her face, but she dabbed at them with the handkerchief he had given her earlier.

"I understand, Miss Barlow. I will do my very best to reach her in the meantime."

"I know it's hard, sir, but please don't let anybody be unkind to her. Underneath all of this, my mother is a good woman, a kind and caring woman who has never hurt a living soul her entire life."

"You strike me as a clever young woman, Miss Barlow, one who ought not to be lied to. So, I won't lie to you and pretend that cruelty doesn't exist in places such as this... because it does. Sometimes it is the other inmates, deranged and unable to help themselves, and sometimes it is the staff. I am just one doctor here of several, and rather a new one at that. I do what I can for my own patients, but it is not always possible for me to have sight of them all day long."

"Thank you for your honesty, Dr Winchester. Thank you for your kindness, for I hadn't expected to find any here today and so you have surprised me. I won't rest easy, I know that, but I shall certainly rest easier than I would have done had I not met you."

"Mrs Barlow, Mrs Barlow?" Dr Winchester smiled before turning his attention upon her mother. "Your daughter is here, Mrs Barlow. Daisy is here," he said, and stared intently at Vera, waiting for her to react. When she did not, he turned to smile apologetically at Daisy.

"I'm sure it will take time, Dr Winchester," Daisy said, suddenly wanting to make him feel better, to take a little pressure from him, for the man clearly carried the burden of kindness for more than one employee at the Lancaster Moor asylum.

When the time came for Daisy to take her leave, it was both an upset and a relief to walk out through the great doors of the asylum. She wanted to run, to be away from the sounds of the screams and wails, the disordered minds of the deranged. At the same time, however, she couldn't bear to leave her mother behind, to have her housed in such an awful place.

Dr Winchester was young and kind, but he was the only one of such a disposition she had seen throughout her entire visit.

She hurried along the path to the gate in the wall, not bothering to let her eyes stray to the lawns and the flowers; they wouldn't lift her spirits now. Quietly thanking the man who opened the gate for her, she quickened her step, running away in every sense. If only all the rest of her problems could be left behind her, locked in a room for somebody else to deal with whilst she ran and ran.

When she finally reached the railway station, hot and breathless, she paid for her ticket and made her way out to the platform. She sat on an iron bench, staring at the rail tracks below. If only she had the strength required to jump down from the platform and simply lay there, waiting for a train to come, waiting for it all to be over.

CHAPTER SEVEN

"Now, I need to come in and inspect the premises, Daisy, you know that. I've been as kind as I can be, as patient as I can be, but there's only so long you can drag out this whole business and expect to be let off lightly." Joe Hamill, the landlord her mother had so regularly decried behind his back, pushed his way past her and into the room.

"I suppose you've heard what happened to my mother," Daisy said, hovering by the still-open door.

"Yes, I heard she lost her marbles in the middle of the mill and tried to kill somebody!" he said, and unbelievably let out a great peal of laughter, clearly entertained by the whole thing.

"Don't you care at all, Mr Hamill?"

"What's it to me? She's not my mother, she's yours. All I care about is getting my rent in on time, nothing more than that. As long as you keep this place nice and hand me my coins when I come for them, the rest of your life isn't any of my business, and I don't care to make it that way. Cry on somebody else's shoulder, Daisy, there's no room on mine."

"I wasn't trying to cry on your shoulder... I wouldn't. I just don't think it's very nice of you to laugh at my mother's suffering, that's all." Daisy hated him, so much so that she wanted to lift the fire poker and strike him with it. How dare he think that it was her business to keep this place nice when it was nothing but a peeling health hazard in the first place?

"Well, you and your ma should have thought about that before you let her put on her fine performance. If folks don't want to be laughed at for being mad, then best they act sane, isn't that right?"

"You've seen the room now, and you can see that it is as tidy as always." Daisy wanted him gone.

"This bit hasn't been swept very well."

"If I swept this room from morning till night without stopping, Mr Hamill, there would still be peelings of paint from the ceiling which drop all the time. Sometimes it is like snow in here, so I'm sure you can see it is no fault of mine."

"All right, all right, don't get your knickers in a twist!" he said crudely. "Let's have the rent then, I can't stand here all day wasting my time. It's a Sunday after all, isn't it? God's day, and here I am working my fingers to the bone collecting rent."

It was on the tip of her tongue to ask what on earth he would know about God. However, she kept her thoughts to herself, knowing that it would do her no good to lose her temper now.

"Here you go," she said, holding out the coins, dropping them into his open palm.

"I must admit, I didn't think you'd be able to keep paying the rent. The pay at the mill must be all right after all... if one little wage is enough to keep you going. Maybe they are paying you too much," he went on, laughing.

"They pay a pittance, Mr Hamill," Daisy said, feeling her mouth go dry; was now the time to tell him that she wouldn't be able to pay in full and on time the following week?

"Well, as long as I get what's owed me, what do I care?"

"This is the last of my mother's savings. She used to keep a few coins in a tin under the floorboards, you see. That's how I've been paying you the last few weeks, Mr Hamill."

"Here we go! Here we blooming go!" he said, his hands flying to his hips, his head shaking vigorously from side to side, although surprisingly not vigorously enough to move one strand of his dreadful greasy hair. It was stuck to his scalp, it was stuck to the side of his face and stuck to his forehead.

"I don't know what to do, Mr Hamill. I'm sure my mother will be back soon, perhaps we could owe it to you?"

"Back soon? From the bleeding funny farm?" he said and let out a loud boom of completely unamused laughter. "Once they're in, they're in! That old lady of yours is going to be foaming at the mouth for the rest of her days, not out and back at the mill paying me the money I'm owed. No, I'm not a charity!" he said, and Daisy wondered why it was that people who survived only because of the poor, perpetually told them that they weren't a charity.

Without paupers, Mr Hamill would get no rent whatsoever for the filthy, rundown housing he provided. Without mill workers, Mr Wainwright wouldn't earn a penny to keep him tall and broad and well fed. Perhaps it was the paupers who were providing the charity for men such as these.

"No," Daisy said, staring up at the peeling paint on the ceiling, wondering what move to make next.

"Mind you, we can always come to some arrangement," he said, his voice changing, becoming something more friendly.

"Oh, yes?" Daisy said, suddenly excited to be getting the first break in her circumstances for what felt like a lifetime. "But what arrangement?"

"Now, don't you come it all innocent with me, girl, I know you know what I'm talking about." He was scowling at her now, and slowly the penny dropped, Daisy knew how he wanted the rent to be paid, what currency she must use.

"Oh, oh, no, I couldn't," Daisy began to back away instinctively as if he might hurt her now.

"I don't see how you think yourself in a position to be so picky, girl! You needn't look at me like that, you could do a lot worse."

"I'm sorry, I didn't mean to offend you, Mr Hamill, it's just that I've never... well, I couldn't. I'm sorry, I just couldn't."

"Oh, I get it, you're just shy!" he said, brightening as if this somehow meant that he wasn't a foul, disgusting, greasy-haired man whom Daisy would rather die than have him touch her.

"But I've paid the rent this week, haven't I? I've paid the rent," she said, keen to remind him that, as it stood, she didn't owe him a single thing.

"But you won't be able to pay next week, will you?" the landlord went on, clearly seeing a bright side now to not being paid. What a foul creature he was!

"No, but I am only thirteen years old, Mr Hamill," she said, trying to make him feel ashamed, trying to appeal to his better nature... if he had one.

"Thirteen years old is plenty old enough, Daisy.

There's girls out there earning their living that way, day in, day out, and from a lot younger than you are now. Now, I'm not one of them strange ones. I don't go in for little kids, never have been like that, never will," he said, straightening his spine and raising his chin as if proudly defending himself. "I mean, I would never have gone for that sister of yours, even though you were twins. She was pretty enough, just like you, but far too small. She was like a child, the shape of her, but you..." he said, and suddenly looked Daisy up and down, his eyes lingering over her curves, his tongue running over his bottom lip. "You ain't no child. So, don't come it with me. Thirteen is plenty old enough, and if you haven't got no other way to pay, then that's what you'll have to do. If not, well," he said and motioned his head towards the door. "You'll be out; out on your ear, that's what!"

"But I don't owe you anything now, Mr Hamill. I've paid, and you've inspected the room. As you said, it's Sunday, you have better things to do than be here." Daisy was shaking from head to foot but in anger. How dare he talk about Janet that way, when she had suffered and died the way that she had?

"You won't get the money for next week; I know you won't. Not just you all on your own in the world, your sister dead, your ma in the nuthouse, and your old pa God knows where! No, you won't have the money," he said, rubbing his hands together, already looking forward to it as if it were a done deal. "I will be seeing you next Sunday, Daisy. You just make sure you're here ready for my visit," he said and ended their conversation by winking at her.

Daisy had never felt more humiliated, and she had never felt more alone in all her life. For a moment, she was angry with her mother; how could she let go of reality when she still had a daughter here on the earth, alive, one who very much needed her? How could she have turned her back on Daisy that way?

As the week had progressed, Daisy had been able to think of nothing else but the circumstances she now found herself in. She wanted to mourn Janet, to worry about her mother, but there wasn't room for that now. As far as Daisy was concerned, she was in mortal danger; if she was forced to lay down with that dreadful man just for the roof over her head, she knew she couldn't go on living. Her mother and sister would have to wait their turn to tear her heart to shreds, Daisy had thinking to do.

She had decided immediately that she would never set eyes on Joe Hamill again as long as she lived. When he appeared on Sunday, it would be to find the room empty, her things gone, no sign of the Daisy he wanted to abuse.

Of course, she would have to leave the area entirely, knowing that Joe Hamill would find her and likely beat her for not paying the last week's rent. To leave the area would mean to leave her job, but she wasn't quite as upset by that as she ought to have been. It sickened her to have to turn up every day and stare at the loom inside which her beloved twin sister had lost her life. Whatever she did in the future, however bad things got, at least she would never have to set eyes on that loom, that dreadful roller beam, ever again.

Daisy worked only until Friday, for Friday was the day on which the workers were paid. There would be no point in her turning up on Saturday when she was leaving for good and would never get her pay for it. She wasn't a charity, after all. So, she had decided that Saturday was the day that she would leave. She would walk away from her home, from the mill, and she would get on a steam train to Lancaster, never once looking back at Burnley.

On Saturday morning, she did just that. With her pittance of a wage, not to mention a couple of coins she had saved to put towards the rent that she had now decided not to pay, she set off. The coin would at least get her to Lancaster and give her enough money for a boarding house for a day or two whilst she looked for work. That was her plan. She would, at least, be closer to her mother. If she could see her once a week, just as Dr Winchester had suggested, perhaps Vera would be well again. Daisy dreamed of her coming out of the Lancaster Moor Asylum. Together, they would look after each other. She was not a child anymore.

However, Daisy knew she couldn't leave Burnley without saying goodbye to her sister, and so she made her way to the churchyard. Slowly, she made her way to the far corner. It was where the large pauper pits were dug. What would she find? The thought was too much and slowed her footsteps even more. Would she be better to remember Janet as she was? Alive and happy, the cheeky child who always saw the best in everything?

It didn't matter, she had to see her and her feet walked of their own accord until she found herself there. Letting out a great breath, she was relieved to find that the pit her sister had been thrown into just four weeks before was now covered. There was, of course, no headstone for any who laid beneath, but there was at least a crudely fashioned wooden cross. It pierced the earth, marking the last resting place of the poor of Burnley.

From the other side of the churchyard, she had picked a single tiny daisy. Now, she laid it on the earth at the part of the plot she thought Janet had been thrown into. She had been so devastated and shocked at the time of Janet's silent funeral that she couldn't be entirely sure, but she was as close as she could be.

Daisy crouched as she set the little flower down, talking in almost a whisper.

"Janet, I'm so sorry, but I have to go. Mama is so ill, she misses you so much, and I can't carry on here by myself. I will think of you every day for the rest of my life. You will always be the other half of me, the beating heart of my body. And I'll never stop loving you, my dear, sweet, funny Janet. I'll never stop missing you. All I have to leave you with is this daisy. I leave it so that you might know it's there, you might know it was *this* Daisy, your beloved Daisy, who left it for you. Rest in peace, Janet. I don't know when I'll be back again," she finished whispering, her throat almost closed with emotion, as tears rolled down her face. "I have to go. I have to get the train to Lancaster. I love you."

CHAPTER EIGHT

*D*aisy had managed to secure work with surprising speed. She had only to pay for one night's accommodation at the boarding house, for she had found herself work in service the very next day. Although Janet's old clothes had been too small to be any good to her, she still had her mother's Sunday best. It was, albeit a little big, but in good condition and suited her. She looked neat and tidy, her hair tied back, her body scrupulously clean, and so the housekeeper who interviewed her took her on immediately.

"And you can read, can you? Read and write?" the housekeeper asked, although it was clear that Daisy had the job.

"I can read better than I can write, Miss. I was sent to a ragged school with my sister when we were both little, but then my father... well, he died and wasn't able to look after us anymore, and my sister and I had to work instead. But I kept up with it as much as I could. If I find a discarded newspaper, I am able to read it." She couldn't bear to tell the woman that her father had run away with his lover. Though the little lie caused her a stab of guilt, it was much better to say he was dead, for was that not as good as true?

"Very well, not that a scullery maid will be called upon to do much reading and writing, but you never know," Mrs Pearson said as she nodded. "Now, I wouldn't normally take on a girl without any experience, but if you've worked in a mill all your life, you will know what a good hard day's work is, I have no doubt of that."

"Yes, Mrs Pearson, they were long days, and the work was hard. But I worked in the mill from the time I was seven years old until now. Six years, a little longer even, and they never had cause to find fault with me."

"Then I shall put you on a few day's trial, to begin with. If you work hard for me this week, there will be a permanent position here for you. It's a big house, even though it doesn't much look it from the outside. Also, Sir Frederick and Lady Bowland have very high standards, and it will go in your favour if you try to stick to those standards."

"I will do whatever I have to, Mrs Pearson."

"Good girl, good girl. Now then, you won't be wanting to work in that good dress, will you? Do you have something else in that bag of yours?" She was almost kind in her ways.

"Yes, I have my work dress, Mrs Pearson."

"All right then, I'll show you to a room in the servants' quarters. Now, you'll have to share, mind you, with three other girls, but it's warm enough, and it's a roof over your head. Come on, let's get you settled in and get you changed, I need you to start working right away."

Daisy was thrilled to have somewhere to work, and a place which came with accommodation to boot. She knew that she would be paid poorly if she was even paid at all, but at least she didn't have to fear the landlord knocking down the door. She shuddered, she could forget about him demanding she paid him in any way possible.

As she followed along behind Mrs Pearson, Daisy smiled to herself, imagining Joe Hamill's face when he turned up at the room just an hour or two from now to find her gone. He would have lost a week's rent and not even have Daisy there to take his pleasure of her. It served him right!

"Right, this is your room," Mrs Pearson said, opening the door and leading her into a large square room. It was spartan, but not excessively so.

The first thing Daisy did was look up, staring at the ceiling. A big smile spread across her face when she saw that the paintwork, whilst not entirely fresh, was certainly still clinging to the plaster. There was no sign of it peeling away.

"What are you looking at, child?" Mrs Pearson asked, studying her with interest.

"Nothing, Mrs Pearson. It's a lovely room, really," Daisy said, wanting to appear to be every bit as grateful as she was.

She didn't care that she had to share this room with

three other girls, strangers, it just didn't matter. She was safe, she had survived, and her morals had remained intact. She was close to her mother, and with luck, she would at least have a little time off every week to go and visit, to help her back to health.

All in all, Daisy felt a little proud of herself. She was still in pain, she would still have given anything for life to go back to what it was, the life she had shared with her mother and sister. But Daisy hadn't let go of reality, she could see it all too clearly. There wasn't time for her to dream of what might have been, only what might be. This was her life now, and she had been brave enough to make the changes all by herself.

"Come on then, get yourself changed, and I'll see you back in the kitchen in five minutes, ready and raring to begin your day." Mrs Pearson said, and Daisy smiled and nodded vigorously.

"Yes, Mrs Pearson."

Daisy was dreaming of her weekly visits to her mother. The improvement was tiny, imperceptible even, but she was convinced it was there. The visits were always a happy time. She would talk to her mother and often Doctor Winchester would pop in and see her.

The man was a dream, always happy and optimistic. They would spend a little time discussing her mother and he never talked down to her. Once or twice he had even invited her for tea; of course, Daisy couldn't stay long but she loved those visits the most. A smile crossed her face, she was so happy in her new life. If only her mother would recover life would be complete.

"Hello, who are you then?" The jaunty male voice behind her sounded young and cultured. It could only be Sir Frederick and Lady Bowland's son, Timothy.

Instantly nervous, Daisy got to her feet, turned around and curtsied.

"I'm Daisy, sir, Daisy Barlow."

"Hello, Daisy Barlow, I'm Timothy Bowland." He

was grinning from ear to ear and Daisy thought he looked very pleasant. He was a very handsome young man, perhaps no older than seventeen or eighteen, with dark blond hair and brown eyes. He was tall and the sort of slender that would undoubtedly fill out in the next year or two.

"There's no need to look so terrified, I don't bite," he said and laughed when Daisy simply stood with her hands by her sides not knowing what to do or say next.

"I'm sorry, sir," she said and curtsied again.

"Well, now you look more terrified. Perhaps I shouldn't have interfered." He was laughing, a pleasant, open sort of a laugh. "How long have you worked here, Daisy?"

"Almost a year, sir."

"Why have I never seen you before?"

"I have been a scullery maid all year, ever since Mrs Pearson took me on."

"Ah, and now you have been promoted to work above stairs?"

"Only in the very early morning, sir. Mrs Pearson says she'll see how I get on setting the fires before the family get up, and if I do all right at it, she might have me do a little dusting in the rooms."

"I must admit to not knowing much about what goes on below stairs, my dear Daisy, but I rather think that you have been promoted very early from scullery maid to housemaid. Well done, you! You must have worked very hard, indeed." He looked so friendly that Daisy couldn't help but warm to him. Perhaps all rich people were not the same after all.

"I work as hard as I can, sir."

"You've come over from East Lancashire, I think. Your accent gives you away," he said and laughed. "No, don't look ashamed, I adore a Burnley or Blackburn accent. Which is it?" He was still smiling, and now Daisy was smiling back.

"Burnley, sir."

"I have been to Burnley once or twice. I rather liked it, surrounded by hills and what have you. I think I am right in saying that there are far more people in extraordinary poverty there than there are here in Lancaster."

"Yes, living in extraordinary poverty, but also working all day every day."

"Were you very poor, Daisy?"

"Yes, I was. I was poor, but I have worked almost every day since I was seven years old. In the mill, sir."

"Do you prefer being in service to being in the mill?"

"I think so. I mean, there's less chance of being killed in service, sir."

"I must admit to being awfully glad that your life is not so in danger here as it was in Burnley. I often think the world is a much nicer place for having very industrious, very pretty young ladies in it." He grinned, and it was somewhere between boyish and utterly daft. "Tell me how old are you?"

"I am fourteen."

"I remember being fourteen. If I'm honest, I wouldn't mind being fourteen again." He was trying to make her laugh, she knew it, but Daisy couldn't help but think that his life at fourteen years old was undoubtedly a very different story from her own life. Perhaps it was easy to long for a particular time in your life when it hadn't been filled with drudgery and poverty.

"Well, you have fallen silent again, my dear. I can see that I am going to have to work on you to have you see me as a friend," he said and amusingly narrowed his eyes as if in the deepest thought. "Which means I'm going to have to wake up at the crack of dawn every day like I did today if I am to have any hope of finding you at your work above stairs."

"Yes, sir," Daisy said, hardly daring to believe that there was a person in this world who wanted to be her friend.

"I will see you tomorrow, Daisy Barlow." He bowed as if she were a fine lady, and it made Daisy laugh.

Perhaps, after more than a year of heartbreak and hard work, life might hold some bright corners for her after all.

CHAPTER NINE

"*I* don't like to send you out when it looks as if the weather is going to take a turn, Daisy," Mrs Pearson said as the two of them stood just outside the door which served as the servants' entrance. She was looking up at the sky, scowling at the black clouds as if that might make them retreat.

"I don't mind at all, Mrs Pearson. I'm sure if I get wet, I will dry out, and I know you need the meat from the farmer in Overton for tonight's dinner party. If I take the pathway through the marsh, I'll be quicker. I should only be gone a couple of hours." Daisy liked Mrs Pearson very much, for the housekeeper had always been kind to her. It made her more determined to work hard and do whatever Mrs Pearson needed her to do.

"Well, mind you move along quickly, Daisy, because I don't think this is just a little bit of rain, I think it's more of a storm." Mrs Pearson patted her arm. "If it starts to look bad, you just come right back, do you hear me?"

"Yes, Mrs Pearson."

As Daisy set off, she was surprised to find Timothy Bowland hovering about the front of the house. He was grinning at her, as he always did, and gave her a little wave to set her on her way. Perhaps he was going somewhere with his parents and waiting for the carriage to be brought round. If only she could go to Overton in the carriage instead of risking being soaked through to the skin on foot.

Daisy waved back, she had become more and more comfortable with Timothy every day. True to his word, he had sought her out most mornings as she went from room to room cleaning out the cold ashes from the fire grates and preparing neat little stacks of coals and wood ready to be lit as soon as the sun came up.

He was such a bright and funny young man with such silly ways that Daisy had begun to wake up in the morning with something of a spring in her step. She knew that the two of them could never be more than friends, not with their vastly differing statuses in the world, but it gave her something nice to dream about. In the last two months, she had thought about Timothy almost every day. She had even secretly imagined herself as his wife, spending every day in comfort and amusement with the carefree, handsome young man.

As she marched along the path through the marsh, once again, Timothy commandeered all her thoughts. In her mind, he would keep her company all the way to Overton and back, and she didn't care at all if it rained or not.

However, when it finally did begin to rain, with Daisy only halfway back to the Bowland's house in Lancaster, it was just as Mrs Pearson had feared. It wasn't just a simple case of rain, for the gale flying up the Lune Estuary was almost enough to lift her off her feet.

The sky had turned so dark, so black, that it was almost as night-time, and Daisy tried to quicken her step. However, carrying the heavy piece of meat made it difficult to move much quicker. Daisy quickly found herself soaked through. The rain became torrential, and she could hardly see a hand in front of her face.

In the end, wanting some respite from the appalling conditions, she dropped down from the pathway and sloshed across the marshland to an abandoned brick building. It was a building that would undoubtedly have been used for sheep in the days before the River Lune had begun to encroach too heavily upon the land for sheep to be grazed there.

The wooden door was all but rotten, but it gave easily, and Daisy darted inside. There was old hay all over the place, but it looked clean enough, and Daisy settled herself down in a part of the little sheep barn that didn't leak and wasn't wet.

Her hair was soaked through, and the bun at the back of her head weighed heavily. She pulled out the pins and shook her hair out, hoping that it might dry a little as she sat there. Her clothes, however, were another matter. Daisy was certain that they wouldn't be dry until she removed them and hung them before the fire back in the servants' quarters.

She felt cold, shivering as she sat, wondering how long the storm would last before she could set off again. Above all things, she hoped that she could get the piece of meat back to Mrs Pearson in time. She didn't want to let her down, not for a minute.

"My goodness! This is a hell of a day, isn't it?" Timothy Bowland's sudden appearance made her cry out in surprise. He'd burst in through the door, shaking his head vigorously, almost like a dog, before closing the door behind him.

"Mr Bowland, what are you doing here?" Daisy asked, getting quickly to her feet.

"When the sky looked blacker still, I thought it might be a good idea to set off in search of you. Mrs Pearson had every cause to be concerned, and I thought that you might be glad of a little company to get you home again."

She was surprised to realise that he had listened in on her conversation with Mrs Pearson earlier that day. Well, she was glad he had!

"I certainly am, sir. I should have listened to Mrs Pearson in the first place, I think. I must admit, I hadn't expected it to come down as hard as this."

"And there's a fair gale picking up now. It always whips along the estuary off the sea when we have a storm."

"I wonder when it will stop?"

"I think it might be a while yet. I think the best thing we can do is try to dry off our things, Daisy. There's no sense in us sitting here in soaking wet clothes whilst we wait for a chill to invade our very bone marrow. Look, there are some hooks up here on the wall, we can hang our clothes from them and wait for them to dry a little bit. They won't dry much, but at least we won't be wrapped in sodden fabric."

"Mr Bowland, I couldn't possibly take off my clothes." Daisy felt suddenly, very embarrassed.

"Goodness me, not all the way!" Timothy said and started to laugh. "You have a full-length slip on, don't you?" he asked, embarrassing her even more with his question.

"Yes, sir," she said, blushing violently.

"Then, it is settled. I do not want to be responsible for you becoming sick when it might have been avoided. Come along, I shall go first if it makes you feel any better."

A lthough her slip was damp, it wasn't quite as sodden as her dress and cloak. Daisy was cold, her shivering taking the edge off her embarrassment.

"Are you very cold?" Timothy asked, sitting down beside her. He had removed only his boots and his shirt, for his trousers had been well protected by the long coat which was now hanging on the hook beside Daisy's dress and shawl.

Daisy hadn't been able to look at him, not openly, not whilst his chest was bare. Her eyes flicked only surreptitiously to him, her mind trying to deny to her heart that he was such a fine-looking young man.

"Yes, I am quite cold."

"Here, let's pile up some of this hay and try to keep warm." He immediately began to scoop the dry hay into something that finally resembled a bird's nest. "Come on, we should be warm in here," he said, reaching for her hand and drawing her towards him.

They sat side by side in their little nest of hay, Timothy's arm around her shoulder. His skin felt strangely warm against her bare arms, and she couldn't deny that the contact of another human being was something that she had missed greatly without her mother and sister in her life.

"Does that feel any better?" he asked, whispering the words into her ear.

"Yes," she said and could feel her heart pounding.

Suddenly, he laid his hand on her face and tilted her chin so that she was looking up at him. He smiled at her, and she knew that he was going to kiss her. But for all her dreams, when the kiss finally happened, Daisy knew that it couldn't. She pulled away a little, looking down apologetically.

"Sir, this cannot be. I am just a maid, and you are the son of Sir Frederick and Lady Bowland." Her voice sounded tiny, tremulous.

"Just one more kiss," he said, holding her more firmly and pressing his lips over hers rather hard. Daisy cried out and try to pull her head away but could not. She pushed her hands against his chest, levering him away, but what she saw in his eyes once she had done so was something that she had not seen in him before. He looked angry and intense, and Daisy began to feel afraid.

"No, please don't," Daisy said, tears rolling down her face.

"We're friends, aren't we? You must know how well I like you, Daisy. You look so soft, so pretty, I just want to..." He didn't finish the sentence, he just lunged at her.

He had thrown her back into the hay and was kissing her so hard that it hurt. Daisy struggled beneath him, her fists pounding away at his shoulders, her feet kicking. However hard she kicked and pounded, the tighter he held her. She could feel his hands dragging her slip up out of the way before fumbling with his own trousers to free himself.

When he finally forced himself inside her, Daisy screamed. How could this be happening? How could the young man she had liked so well and trusted be hurting her this way? Humiliating her, taking what was not freely given! Her cries, however, did nothing to stop him. Timothy Bowland simply carried on, as if in some sort of trance, until he was finished.

When the rain cleared, it cleared suddenly and instantly gave way to pale-yellow sunshine. The wind had died down, and it was almost as if the storm had never happened. Perhaps that was how Daisy should see the entire day, something that had never happened.

She dressed in her sodden clothes, keeping her eye on the sleeping form of Timothy the entire time. He was half-naked in the hay, sleeping so peacefully that he was almost like a child. Wanting to be away from him, Daisy tied her wet shawl around her shoulders, picked up the meat from the Overton farmer, and crept out the door.

Daisy had been walking hurriedly for more than twenty minutes when he finally caught up with her. She was no more than ten minutes from the house now, and she could have cried, she felt so vulnerable. Why could he not have slept a few more minutes?

Why could she not be far away from him and safe again?

"Wait, Daisy, let's walk back together," Timothy called out in his ordinary friendly manner as he walked along by her side.

Daisy said nothing, not even turning to look at him. Instead, she quickened her pace and stared directly ahead, willing herself to be back at the house in Lancaster.

"Daisy? Daisy, what is it?" he asked as if he had no idea.

"You hurt me. I said *no*, and you went on and did it anyway. You took what I refused to give, and you took it by force."

"Daisy, I thought you liked me," he said, sounding genuinely confused.

"And I thought you liked me."

"I do, otherwise I wouldn't have..."

"Hurt me?" Daisy said, feeling a most exquisite bout of hatred for him.

"I'm sorry, I didn't mean to hurt you. I suppose I just couldn't stop myself."

"You couldn't stop? My goodness, you have just made yourself sound like the victim," she said in a surprisingly calm voice now that they had come off the marsh pathway and were heading into town. There were people around her now, he surely couldn't hurt her with so many to see him do it.

"I hope we can still be friends, Daisy. You know how I like to get up early and spend that time with you whilst you're setting up the fires." He looked upset, like a chastised child.

"We cannot be friends, sir. Friends do not treat each other that way."

"But, Daisy..." There was such an appealing tone to his voice that Daisy was sure that he couldn't even see what he had done wrong.

"You *raped* me. We will never be friends again." Daisy quickened her pace as she marched towards the house.

CHAPTER TEN

*D*aisy had managed to avoid Timothy for more than two months. She had asked Mrs Pearson to keep her below stairs, to return her to her duties as a scullery maid, claiming that she wasn't yet confident. Mrs Pearson had seen through it all, of course, and had asked her time and time again what the matter was.

Daisy knew she could say nothing, for if word of what had happened reached Sir Frederick and Lady Bowland, she would undoubtedly be cast out. The rich could do what they liked, couldn't they?

However, by not telling Mrs Pearson what had happened, eventually, the day came when she was sent to work above stairs again, back to her duties of cleaning out the grates and setting the fires. There was no way she could get out of it without giving Mrs Pearson the details, and so in the end, Daisy had acquiesced.

She had set two of the fires ready before moving on to the library. Every step she took, she felt as if she were looking over her shoulder, dreading the appearance of Timothy Bowland, her attacker. By the time she had reached the library, she had begun to feel safe. Perhaps, over the last two months, he hadn't bothered to get up early and seek her out. Perhaps, now that he had taken what he wanted, he didn't particularly care to see her again. Whatever the reason, she was simply glad that he was not there, and she relaxed a little as she cleaned the ash from the library fire grate.

"It has been an age since I have seen you, Daisy. Where have you been hiding?" As soon as she heard his voice and realised that he was behind her, Daisy was almost overwhelmed by heat and nausea. Just his voice was enough to transport her back to that awful day of pain and humiliation, and it was all she could do to carry on with her work when she wanted to get up and run.

"Daisy, do you not trust me?" he asked, when she looked over her shoulder towards the door, relieved that it was a little ajar.

"No, I do not trust you. I would beg you to leave me alone, Mr Bowland." Her voice was shaky.

"Daisy, I wish I could take it back. It was only my passion for you, that's all. I never meant to hurt you," he said and laid a hand on her shoulder.

Daisy was on her feet in a flash, the fire poker in her hand, held out towards him as she began to back away.

"There's no need for this, I think you know that. I think you know that I wouldn't hurt you."

"You already have, can't you see it? Don't you think about what you did and realise that it was wrong? You have ruined me, Mr Bowland, and you have ruined me against my will. I won't let you do it again, I would rather die." Tears streamed down her face as she continued to hold the fire poker with both hands, raised, ready to strike him.

"Daisy, I have missed you more than I can say. You have no idea how much this has hurt me."

"And you have no idea how much you have hurt me. This was your doing, Mr Bowland, not mine. Please just stay away from me." Daisy stared at him as the tears began to run down his own face. He was feeling sorry for himself, wishing that he hadn't acted the way he had, but it only made her feel more hatred for him.

"I can see that you expect me to forgive you, but I never can. I will never be able to forget that day as long as I live, and I don't believe that you couldn't stop yourself. I don't believe that of *any* man; it is an excuse, and I know it to be an excuse. I will never forgive you." Daisy stopped herself from trying to hurt him further by telling him that his rape of her had come with more consequences than pain and humiliation; Daisy was quite certain that she was with child.

She wanted him to know it, to spend night after night worrying about it the way she did, but she knew she couldn't risk it, not yet. She had to keep herself safe and in her position for as long as she could, for she would be cast out soon enough once her condition became obvious. Much better to keep a hold of her temper and her secret and make the most of the last few months of safety she would ever enjoy again.

"Are we really never going to be friends again?"

"I have never hated anybody more than I hate you, Timothy Bowland. If you come near me again, I will go directly to your mother and tell her what you did to me. Now get out!" she said and took a step towards him, ready to strike him with the fire poker.

And, coward that he was, Timothy Bowland turned on his heels and ran away.

D aisy was only five months along when her condition began to be truly obvious. Mrs Pearson had tried to talk to her about it, but Daisy simply pretended that it wasn't happening, denying that she was with child at all but simply that she was living better now and had gained weight. She knew that Mrs Pearson didn't believe her, as well as she knew that fine woman was also trying to buy her a little time by saying nothing to anybody else.

However, when the butler decided to take his suspicions to Sir Frederick, Daisy was quickly called to stand before his wife, Lady Bowland.

Daisy had only ever been in the drawing room before the family were awake, cleaning out the fire and setting it for the day. It was an awful experience to be taken into the room by Mrs Pearson, to be left standing in front of Lady Bowland as she sat on one of the couches.

"It has been brought to my attention that you are with child, Daisy Barlow, and now that I see with my own eyes, I see that it is true," Lady Bowland said, and Daisy realised that this was the first time they had ever met. She had seen Lady Bowland from afar but had never crossed paths with her above stairs. "Have you nothing to say for yourself?"

Daisy could think of nothing, she simply looked down, feeling almost as humiliated as she had done that day out on the marsh.

"I thought not. Your kind never apologises, do they? You never feel the sense of shame you ought to feel. I suppose that is what separates us, what makes us better than you," Lady Bowland said, and Daisy could feel her humiliation turning to anger.

"You're not better than me, you're not!" Daisy said angrily, raising her head at last and staring directly into her employer's eyes.

"Daisy," Mrs Pearson whispered, beseeching her.

"How dare you?" Lady Bowland's bird-like hands flew to her chest. Once she had gathered herself, her eyes narrowed. "How dare you speak to me that way?"

"And how dare you say that your kind is better than my kind, Lady Bowland? I am in this condition because of one of *your* kind. Yes, that's right! I didn't have a say in the matter. Something was taken from me that I wasn't prepared to give freely, and I think you know exactly what I mean."

"You are claiming some sort of attack?" Lady Bowland said but seemed to be a little nervous now. "Mrs Pearson, you may leave us for the time being," she added hurriedly, and Mrs Pearson turned to leave.

"Your son raped me, Lady Bowland. Timothy

Bowland raped me out on the marshes on the day of the great storm. He followed me, and he took the most dreadful advantage. There, now you know!" Daisy said, taking some little pleasure from having made her declaration loudly, and before Mrs Pearson had managed to leave the room.

"That is a terrible lie, girl, and you will take it back immediately," Lady Bowland said, angry and afraid all at once.

Daisy stared at her, leaning forward, peering into her brown eyes, eyes so like those of her son. There it was, she could see it. Lady Bowland knew that it was true.

"You know," Daisy said, her mouth falling open. "You know him to be capable of it, Lady Bowland. You know he raped me. You know that this child in my belly is your blood, don't you?"

"All I know is that you are a rough, immoral little mill girl who should never have been allowed into my house. You are clearly trying to extort money from us, but who would believe you? Who would believe someone like *you* against someone like my son?" Warming to her theme, Lady Bowland's confidence returned.

Daisy knew, of course, that it was well-deserved confidence. Lady Bowland was right; who would believe Daisy when faced with a fine, bright, and friendly young gentleman like Timothy Bowland? Nobody, that was who.

"Mrs Pearson?" Lady Bowland bellowed in a rather unladylike fashion, drawing the housekeeper back into the sitting room. "This girl is to be dismissed immediately and expelled from this house. In future, you are to be very careful whom you employ, Mrs Pearson. If a single word of this girl's lies is repeated below stairs or anywhere inside or outside of this house, you will be similarly dismissed, and without references, just as this creature is to be. Have I made myself clear?"

"Yes, My Lady," Mrs Pearson said and bowed her head.

"That will be all," Lady Bowland said, turning her head to look away from the girl who was carrying her grandchild.

CHAPTER ELEVEN

*H*er parting with Mrs Pearson had been an emotional one, and that dear woman had given her a few coins to last the week. Even though it was a day that Daisy had always known would come, it all still felt so very shocking in reality. How could a position which had started so well have ended so badly? She wasn't just back to where she had started, she was in a worse state than she had ever been in her life.

There was only one place left for her in this world if she was to at least keep herself and her baby alive for a while. She couldn't go there, however, until she had said her final goodbye to her mother. So, carrying her few possessions, Daisy began the short walk to the Lancaster Moor Asylum.

"You seem a little better today, Mama," Daisy said, repeating the line she always greeted her mother with when she visited her at the asylum.

They always had privacy now, for Vera Barlow no longer shared one of the great cells with so many other women. Being quieter than the rest, she had been billeted in a smaller room with another woman of a similar disposition. Whenever Daisy visited, the other woman was quietly led away by one of the nurses, and she was certain that it was upon the instruction of Dr Winchester himself. Previously, the idea that it might have irritated the sour Sister Ryan had pleased her, but not today. Today was just too awful.

"You still look a little thin, though, Mama. You really must try to eat the food that they give you, you must keep your strength up," Daisy said, feeling tearful as she stared into the blank face and vacant eyes of her mother.

The truth was that Daisy didn't know if her mother had improved or not. At times she thought she had, but now, today, she couldn't be sure. She had stopped rocking herself back and forth over the last year or so, slowly but surely, but sometimes she didn't speak at all. She simply spent her days sitting in a chair staring into space, as if nothing at all happened in her mind anymore. Daisy often wondered where her mother was, what had become of her soul and her sense of self now that her mind was so disordered. She was beginning to think that they would never talk again, not as they had once done. She was beginning to think that her mother was lost forever, and at a time that she needed her the most.

"I don't know how much you understand of what I say, Mama, but I have things to tell you. I need to talk to you of all people, and I have nobody else to pour my heart out to. Truth is, I have to go away, and I don't know if I will ever be back again. No, that's not right, I *do* know. I am to go away, and I know that I will never be back. It breaks my heart, but it's true," Daisy said and reached into the pocket of her dress to take out the handkerchief that she always used. It was the handkerchief that Dr Winchester had given her more than eighteen months before when she had first visited the asylum.

Vera simply stared ahead, giving no sign whatsoever that she had heard a single word that Daisy had uttered. Nonetheless, Daisy continued.

"I was cast out of my position at the Bowland house today, Mama. Please don't be angry with me, it was through no fault of my own. I have worked hard there day in, day out, just as you always taught me to work hard. But something happened, something that was out of my control, something that I couldn't stop. The Bowland's have a son, you see, and he took from me something that I wasn't prepared to give freely. He forced me, Mama. He hurt me so badly and now I have nowhere else to go."

Again, Vera simply stared straight ahead.

"Mama, I am with child, and it is my attacker's child. These are words I never thought I'd say to you, but the life I have led without you and Janet has been so very hard. Nothing is as I thought it would be, and now I am ruined forever, even though Timothy Bowland is to blame, not me." She couldn't go on for a moment, covering her face with her handkerchief and sobbing into it.

"I have nowhere to go, and only a few coins that the housekeeper gave me to survive for a few days. As much as this is not my fault, it's not the child's fault either. I have to do what I can to keep my baby alive, although I know that I won't get a position anywhere now in my condition, not a moral one, at any rate. So, there is only one place for me. If you were here with me now, properly here with me, I think you would have already understood that I must go to the workhouse. If I don't, I will be sleeping on the streets. I will give birth on the streets, and I will probably die there with my child, so there's nothing else for it really."

"Yes, there is." The voice behind her startled her and she turned her head sharply to see that Dr Winchester had silently entered the room. "Forgive me, I should not have eavesdropped, and yet I did. I should have announced my presence, but I was certain that you would have fallen to silence."

"Dr Winchester, you can't tell anybody what you've heard. Nobody would believe it, you see. Everyone would believe a fine young gentleman like Timothy Bowland over somebody like me."

"I believe you. I believe you, and it is clear that Timothy Bowland is anything but a fine young gentleman."

"Thank you, Dr Winchester. Just to have somebody believe me is more than I could have hoped for. I don't want to upset my mother, but I couldn't leave her forever without saying goodbye."

"You will not be leaving her forever at all. Miss Bowland, how far along are you?"

"I think five months, sir."

"Well, I am in need of a maid of all works in my house in Lancaster. It is far away from the centre of town where the Bowland's live, so you need not fear. My house is up by Williamson Park. You know the park, of course?"

"Yes, I walk through it to come here," Daisy said, her heart pounding as she wondered if she was, once again, about to be saved.

"My house is directly opposite the park on Quernmore Road. I shall write you a note, and you are to go directly there and hand the note to Mrs Jenkins, my cook. She will settle you for now, and we shall decide upon your duties when I return this evening. I shall leave you alone whilst I prepare my note. Perhaps you might tell your mother about your changing circumstances. I'm certain that she begins to take in some information, and I wouldn't want her to think you are in the workhouse."

"Thank you, Dr Winchester. I don't have the words to tell you how grateful I am."

"Just explain to your mother, Miss Barlow, and I will see to that note.

As he left the room, Daisy felt her heart soar. This man had been so good to her. There was genuine goodness about him that made her feel safe and loved. Shaking her head at such fanciful thoughts, she explained it all to her mother and as she did a tear ran from her mother's eye and down her cheek.

"Now, you can forget about cleaning the fire grates, my girl, you're too close to your time for that!" Mrs Jenkins said with a hoot of laughter. "It's a wonder you can reach at all over that belly of yours!"

"Mrs Jenkins, you are kind, but I must pull my weight. I still have a month before my time, I want to keep going."

The doctor had quite inaccurately described Mrs Jenkins as his cook, for she was far more than that. A bright and brash Cockney woman from the heart of London, she had travelled with the doctor when he had moved to work in the field of maladies of the mind up north in Lancaster.

As far as Daisy could tell, she was more of a housekeeper who could cook rather than simply a cook. She prepared simple meals for her master, which he seemed to enjoy, leaving much of her day free to perform tasks about the house. She had been pleased to have Daisy by her side, for Dr Winchester had been promising her a little help ever since they had arrived in Lancaster.

"I used to manage before, Daisy, and I'll manage

again. I won't have you hurting yourself, not to prove a point. Dr Winchester knows what a good little worker you are, I've already told him. You don't have to prove it every single day."

"Mrs Jenkins, you're so kind. And the doctor is kind too, I thank the Lord every day for my position here. If it hadn't been for the two of you, I would be in the workhouse now."

"Oh, no, I'm sure you wouldn't," Mrs Jenkins said, but it was clear she was just trying to cheer her up.

"It's all that somebody in my condition can expect."

"Which is a disgrace, Daisy, and not yours. It's the disgrace of the world we live in, this pious little country with its pious little ways."

"You always make me feel better, Mrs Jenkins," Daisy said truthfully. In the two and a half months that she had worked in the doctor's house, she and Mrs Jenkins had never had a cross word between them. The kindly housekeeper-come-cook had simply accepted Daisy's condition without questions or judgements.

"It's time for you to understand that not everything

that happens to you in life is your fault." Mrs Jenkins seemed a little cautious. "Leave the fire, let's go into the kitchen and have some tea. Let's have a few minutes to ourselves before that cheeky stable lad comes bursting in looking for scones."

Daisy followed Mrs Jenkins, relieved to sit down at the large wooden kitchen table and rest for a while. Her child was heavy and, if she was honest, exhausting her.

"Here you go, get that down you," Mrs Jenkins said when she finally made the tea and set a steaming cup down in front of her.

"Thank you, Mrs Jenkins," Daisy said and sipped at it gratefully.

"I know what happened to you, my sweet," Mrs Jenkins said, her sharp Cockney accent seeming suddenly soft and gentle. "You mustn't be angry with the doctor, he's a good man. I think he wanted me to know so that there wouldn't be any misunderstandings. In his own way, he was trying to protect you. Of course, he ought to have known that I wouldn't have taken against you anyway. Still, he's a man, they don't always see things as clearly as we do."

"You know that I was...?" Daisy said, realising that she felt more relieved than angry. She had often wondered what Mrs Jenkins thought of her and her condition.

"Taken against your will? Yes, I know." Mrs Jenkins sat down at the table beside her and laid her big, podgy hand on Daisy's. "It takes an almighty time to get over it as well, Daisy. It will come into your mind again and again, and I'm afraid you'll just have to let it. If you keep batting it away, it won't be going anywhere. It'll just sit there inside of you, waiting for you to take notice of it, turning you mouldy from the inside out. Take it from one who knows," she said, and her kind eyes filled with tears.

"You know what it is like?" Daisy asked, her own throat tight with emotion.

"Before I worked for the doctor, I worked in one of them big, fine houses. Not in Lancaster of course, but right down in London, Kensington, as a matter of fact. I know what the upper classes are like! Them as have never had to work an hour in their lives. Anyway, it was the man of the house. He was a pig, and he lied to his wife, good and proper when I went and told her."

"You told her?"

"Her husband was a rapist, my sweet, the poor woman had a right to know. Mind you, not that it stopped her turfing me out onto the street without a reference. They deny everything, even to themselves, that sort. Anyway, I might not have had a reference, but I wasn't with child either. I was able to carry on, after a fashion, and that was when I went to work for Dr Winchester's father. He was Dr Winchester too, so it's been a little complicated now and again over the years," she said and gave a hearty laugh. "But he's a good man, the young Dr Winchester, just like his father was when he was alive. You might think you've landed on your feet, but you've every right to. You've every right to live in this world and be safe and happy in it, just as much as everybody else. I know it doesn't always work that way, but you're here now, and everything's going to be all right.

"I'm so sorry for what happened to you, Mrs Jenkins. Does it ever go away?"

"I won't lie to you, Daisy. It doesn't go away, no. You don't forget it; you can learn to live with it. You can even be happy, although you might not believe it right now."

"I think I'd believe anything you told me, Mrs Jenkins. Thank you," Daisy said, and turned her palm upward and tightened her fingers around Mrs Jenkins' hand.

CHAPTER TWELVE

"*S*ometimes, familiarity is the very thing to draw the affected mind back into the present. The familiarity of places, people, even occupations. When a mind is in retreat, it is often the commonplace which draws it back to the fore.*" Daisy lifted her head from the book and looked ahead of her. Surely, this was the approach that Dr Winchester was taking with her mother, although the familiarity was simply with herself rather than her old surroundings.

The moment Daisy realised that she wasn't alone in the doctor's study, she gasped and closed the book shut. She certainly hadn't been expecting to see the doctor himself, not so early in the day, and her face turned scarlet.

"Forgive me, Dr Winchester. I shouldn't have touched your things, but the book caught my attention. I'm afraid I became a little engrossed." She felt hot and panic-stricken, suddenly exhausted and wishing that she could sit down.

"It's only a book, Daisy," Dr Winchester said, laughing as he advanced into the room, running a hand through his thick, dark hair. "So, what was it that caught your attention?" He seemed genuinely interested. "And Daisy, do sit down, you look exhausted. Mrs Jenkins has already spoken to me about you doing too much and refusing to relax." He pulled back the chair from his desk and gently pushed her down into it. In a rather relaxed manner, he pushed some of the papers along his desk and sat upon the top.

"It's one of your medical books, sir." She handed him the book, and he nodded and smiled as he took it. "I was just reading about familiarity bringing a person back to themselves. Is that what you're trying to do with my mother?"

"I am. There are a number of medical volumes in print which attempt to cover the subject of mental disorders, but I find this is the best of them. The others can be a little... *cruel*, in their approach. I'm afraid I do not see the benefit of ice-cold baths or electrical shocks. The mind is not always a physical thing, rather it is a concept of sorts, I suppose."

"A concept?" Daisy said, confused.

"Rather like the soul, Daisy. You know it's there, but nobody's ever seen it, have they? The soul, the mind, no surgeon has ever opened a chest or a head and held either of those things in his hands as he might a heart or a bone. I suppose I'm trying to say that the mind is real, but not a physical thing. It not being a physical thing, I have never understood how the application of certain stimuli to the physical body can do anything to help. It is talking, gently trying to understand, that is the key to it all, I'm sure."

"Dr Winchester, I pray every night before I go to sleep, and I always give thanks that my mother is in your care and not some other doctor who might use other methods. Like *stimuli*," she said, trying the word out for size. "I'm sure your kindness is starting to reach her, and I'm so grateful to you."

"We doctors take an oath to do no harm, Daisy, an oath which many of my colleagues seem to forget in their haste to discover something clever and be known throughout the medical world. But, a mental crisis is no place for our egos to reside. It is a place for kindness and caring, a place for understanding and warmth. There, I will never be famous, will I?" He started to laugh, and Daisy smiled at him.

He looked younger when he laughed, even more handsome.

"I'm not sure that being famous is the same as being happy, so perhaps you're better off without fame in the first place, Dr Winchester," Daisy said and was thrilled when he nodded, giving her opinion room and really listening to her.

"Then you are like me, my dear. You wish for happiness more than anything else." His bright blue eyes held hers for a moment, and Daisy felt something that she'd never felt before in her life. She felt the first fluttering of a young woman falling in love.

How different this was from her amused and friendly feelings towards Timothy Bowland before he'd done his very worst and utterly betrayed her. Timothy had been just a boy, a spoiled child who, despite his smiles and jokes, was nothing more than a little monster who had no idea how to control his impulses. But Dr Winchester was a man. He was quiet, thoughtful, and considerate. He cared for people even when his colleagues, everybody around him, thought him foolish. He was a man to fall in love with, even though Daisy knew that, once again, it could never be. He might not be upper-class like the Bowland family, but he was certainly a gentleman and a learned man. And she, for her part, was a barely educated girl from Burnley, a mill worker who was already with child.

No, she would just be grateful for her position, for her safety, and leave her dreaming behind. Where had dreaming got her in the past? Nowhere.

"Is contentment the same thing?" she asked.

"Contentment is a very fine thing, Daisy, but it is not always necessarily happiness. Maybe happiness is what we should strive for; what do you think?" he said and started to laugh.

"Maybe you're right, Dr Winchester," Daisy said and laughed too.

"Then we have a deal, my dear. We shall each of us search for happiness and not be content until we have found it," he said and stuck out his hand as if they were truly making a bargain.

As she took his hand and smiled up into his handsome face, Daisy had the strangest sense that her life was about to change again.

D aisy knew she shouldn't have walked to the asylum that day, not with just days until she was due to give birth, but she had wanted to see her mother so badly.

Vera was sitting in a chair in her room, staring into the little glass jar of wildflowers that Daisy had picked for her. Daisy was sure she saw the beginnings of a smile on her mother's lips from time to time.

As was her habit, Daisy chattered away to her mother as

if she assumed her to understand. She was certain that she didn't, but she needed to talk to her, nonetheless. Even if Vera could not respond, Daisy still needed her.

"Mrs Jenkins continues to be kind to me, Mama. She says that she will help me when the baby comes, even though she's never had a baby of her own. She says that we will have to work it out between us, and if we get stuck, she's sure that Dr Winchester will have the answer." Daisy laughed, softening her gaze as she stared at her mother, so intent upon the wildflowers.

"I think I've started to forget about Timothy Bowland and what he did. It's not my baby's fault, and so I have decided to see this little one as just mine, all mine. My baby, nobody else's."

Vera's attention wandered away from the wildflowers for a moment, and she turned her head to look at Daisy. She began to smile, slowly but surely, and the muscles in her face twitched as if they had needed a little notice to get used to smiling again. Once again, she looked away, back at the flowers, and so Daisy continued.

"The only thing which makes me afraid now, or sad,

really, is the idea that my little baby is going to suffer through life being thought of as a bastard. I can't bear the word, but that's what people will say, isn't it? It's how my child will be treated." It had bothered Daisy for a long time now, ever since her primary concern of safety had been addressed and she had been able to think of other things. "I'll love this child forever. I can't bear the thought of other people treating him or her so badly." Finally, she began to cry.

Wiping her face with the handkerchief that Dr Winchester had given her so long ago, Daisy was surprised when she felt a hand on her swollen belly. She opened her eyes to see that her mother had leaned forward, that it was *her* hand on Daisy's stomach. Vera peeled her hand away and reached up to Daisy's face, wiping away the last of her tears with her fingers. It was something that her beloved mother hadn't done for two years.

"Mama?" Daisy said, the emotions swirling in her chest almost as fervent as her fidgeting baby in her belly.

Her mother turned away again, plucking at the little glass jar of wildflowers. When she turned back,

Daisy could see that she had picked one of them out and was handing it to her.

"It's a Daisy," her mother said, her voice dry and almost unrecognisable, it had been so long since she had used it. "A beautiful little Daisy, just like you."

When the time came for Daisy to leave the asylum, she was in floods of tears. Dr Winchester stepped out of his room and caught hold of her arm gently, leading her into his office.

"Daisy, what's the matter?" he asked, settling her down into the chair by his desk.

"I think I'm happy and sad all at once. My mother is getting better, isn't she?"

"Yes, I truly believe that she is."

"She gave me this," she said and held out the tiny Daisy. "She said it was a beautiful little Daisy, just like me."

"I was so sure she would begin to recognise you bit by bit. This is wonderful news, Daisy. It is wonderful progress," he said, and his handsome face seemed to light up. He really did care, she could not only see it, but she could feel it. "Why are you crying? I mean, why are you sad at the same time as you are happy?"

"Oh, it was nothing. It was just something I was talking to my mother about."

"Something you don't want to tell me?" he said and gave her a coaxing smile.

"I don't like to keep things from you, Dr Winchester, you've been so kind."

"I might have been kind, Daisy, but you don't owe me any explanations. You work hard, you don't owe me anything. You don't owe anybody anything, do you understand?"

"I was just worried about my baby, Doctor. I know everyone will call my child a bastard, and I can't bear it. Life is hard enough without that. I suppose I wanted to say it out loud, to tell my mother and get some comfort from her. I suppose I was surprised when she was able to give that comfort, but I'm not sure she understood what I was saying, not really."

"She will understand. In time, she will understand." He cleared his throat and suddenly seemed a little awkward. "But I understand now, Daisy. I'm here, I'm listening, and I understand."

"You're so kind to everyone, when do you have time to care about yourself?" she said, dabbing at her eyes with the handkerchief she had looked after so carefully for so long.

"I think I'm thinking about myself right now, Daisy." Again, he seemed awkward.

"How so?"

"I want to ask you to marry me, my dear. The thing is, I'm almost certain that you would see it as my rescuing you, saving you from all your fears about your child. And, I'd probably get away with it too, wouldn't I? But I don't want to lie to you, Daisy. I've never lied to you before."

"Marry me?" Daisy said, her mouth falling open, her eyes wide.

"That's right, I want to marry you. Not to rescue you, Daisy, but to rescue me. You see, I've never been in love before, not until now, and it's all very unsettling. It's been wonderful having you at the house, but I think it's given me something to think about. I never realised I was lonely until you came into my life."

"And are you lonely now?"

"Not as lonely as I have been, but lonelier than I might be if you would agree to be my wife."

"You're a gentleman, Dr Winchester, and I'm just a girl from Burnley, a mill worker, nothing more."

"You are the strongest human being I have ever encountered in my life. You had to take care of yourself in the worst of circumstances, and you survived. You not only survived, but you did so whilst still caring for your mother. You made sure you saw her at every opportunity. And when the very worst happened, you had the strength to decide to take yourself off to the workhouse so that your child might live. I have never seen such strength in any man or woman, much less somebody as young as you. As young and as beautiful as you, Daisy. Put aside any fears about class and status, these aren't things which trouble me."

"I've fallen in love with you too, Dr Winchester, but I never thought I would be able to say it out loud. I never thought you'd feel the same way."

"Well, I do. I love you, Daisy. I want you to be my wife, by my side, forever. And I will take care of your child as my own, no different from the other children we'll have in the future. What do you say, Daisy? Will you do it? Will you marry me?"

"Of course, I will. Of course, I'll marry you," she said, and got to her feet, throwing herself into his arms. When he kissed her, it was truly a kiss. It was the first time she had ever been kissed, for it had been given, not taken.

This was the beginning of life finally; this was how life was supposed to be lived.

EPILOGUE

"*S*he fair wears me out, that little one. She has enough energy and cheek for an army, and only four years old! You certainly named her right when you named her Janet, and that's the truth!" Vera Barlow gave a great sigh before settling herself down into one of the wrought iron chairs on the terrace. "Be careful, Janet! You're too little to climb trees!" she called out, and her granddaughter hurtled towards her, her arms outstretched.

"She's so like Janet, Mama. She talks all day and half of the night, and she never cries but is always smiling and laughing. I knew the moment I set eyes on her she'd be just like Janet." With her two-year-old son on her knee, Daisy reached out to tuck Janet's wayward hair behind her ear.

Dr Henry Winchester had married Daisy as soon as the child had been born, for there had not been the time before. The day after he had proposed to her, Daisy had gone into labour. Janet had been delivered safely, thanks to Mrs Jenkins and Henry.

"And now another one is on the way. I'm so glad I'm here now with you, my little chicken, I'm so glad I'm able to help you at last." Vera Barlow blinked rapidly, and Daisy reached out to touch her face.

"You have been home so long now, Mama, helping me every day. My little Janet is as she is because she is raised by the same wonderful woman who raised her namesake. I couldn't have managed it without you, Mama." Daisy felt a little tearful, but then she was always a little emotional at this stage of her pregnancy.

She was hoping for another girl this time, somebody for little Janet to concentrate her attention on. Little Henry, at just two years old, often grew exasperated with his older sister, although it was clear that the two loved one another very much indeed.

"I thought I'd find you all here! Where better on such a fine day as this?" Henry was home from work, striding across the lawn and smiling at his wife and mother-in-law. "Steady on, Janet," he said when his daughter ran at full speed into his legs. He lifted her high into the air, spinning her around until she let out delighted squeals. "Did you miss your papa?"

"I did, Papa, I did!" Janet said, clinging on to his neck and raining sweet little kisses down on his nose.

Henry had done exactly as promised and taken little Janet into his heart as his own daughter. Even when his son had come along two years later, Daisy had never seen any difference in his treatment of the children. They never spoke of the Bowland's anymore; none of it seemed to matter now. They were their own little family, soon to swell to an even greater number.

Daisy looked around her with a true feeling of happiness. Everything had finally come good, after a life that Daisy could still hardly believe had been so hard. However, if she could have one wish come true, it would be to have her Janet back, her beloved twin, the other half of herself. She had returned to Burnley, of course, to tell Janet that everything was all right, that she was happy, that she had a family now and that their mother was well again. And Henry, fine man that he was had paid for a headstone to be set in the ground in the place that Daisy had remembered her sister being laid to rest.

Their mother lived with them now, having been released from the asylum when baby Janet was just a year old. She had come on in leaps and bounds when Daisy had, despite the scornful glances of Sister Ryan, taken the infant in to see her grandmother every single day. The death of one Janet had put Vera Barlow into the asylum, and the birth of another had brought her out of it again.

"Well, Mrs Jenkins says that if we are not all in the dining room in the next five minutes, the dinner will be spoiled. Dramatic, I know, but she seemed to mean it," Henry said and, still carrying Janet, waited for the ladies to get to their feet.

He followed them into the house, catching up with his wife and stealing a kiss before they went inside.

"I would call you a thief, Henry, but it was a very nice kiss," Daisy said and smiled at her husband.

"I am a thief, but an unashamed one!" he said and

started to laugh. "You look beautiful, my love," he said, holding tightly to little Janet with one strong arm as he laid the palm of his hand on his wife's swollen belly. Baby Henry began to wriggle in Daisy's arms to get his father's attention and was rewarded with a little kiss on his chubby knee.

"I'm very blessed to have such a wonderful family," Daisy said, pausing outside the open morning room door and looking up into Henry's handsome face.

"I never thought I'd get this far in life," Henry said. "I mean being happy, being a married man with two wonderful children and one on the way. I love you, Daisy. I'll always love you."

"And I will always love you, Henry."

Daisy looked on at her family and knew she had found peace and true happiness.

Thanks for Reading

I love sharing my Victorian Romances with you and have several more waiting for my editor to approve.

As a member of my <u>Newsletter</u>, you will be the first to find out when my books are available. Join now, and I will send you The Foundling's Despair FREE.

I want to thank you so much for reading this book. Read on for a sneak preview of The Lost Nightingale

THE LOST NIGHTINGALE PREVIEW

Anna Bailey crept through the hushed crowd. She was small enough to ease her way, weaving back and forth, without causing a fuss. It was easy when Lucy Lawrence was flying through the air; the crowd were too mesmerised to pay much heed to the scruffy girl sneaking her way to the front.

The big top of *Gerrity's Unbelievable Show* was average for a travelling circus of their standard. It was large enough to accommodate seating for those who could afford a few extra coins to sit in comfort, with a pit area for the masses who couldn't. Anna always crept through the pit area. If she tried to wander through the seating, Mr Gerrity might have seen her and lost his famous temper; famous among the performers, at any rate. For anyone paying to see the show, Mr Gerrity was a fine-looking man with a big sense of humour and an even bigger laugh. It seemed that everything, absolutely everything, was a part of the show, even Mr Gerrity's character.

Finally, Anna could see what she had come to see. Lucy, her knees hooking her to the bar of the trapeze, her arms spread wide, flew through the air. The crowd all looked up as one, reminding Anna of the countless times she'd watched migrating birds turning together. She'd always wondered what force drew them to act in unison. Of course, looking at the tipped heads of all around her, Anna needn't wonder why. Lucy was a true wonder, and as far as Anna was concerned, the star of the show.

"With no safety net, she flies high above the treacherous ground, that earth ready and waiting to swallow her up!" Mr Gerrity roared, whipping the crowd up into a frenzy.

Anna despised his additions to what should have simply been a thing of beauty. She despised the way he dangled death as a possibility; a possibility the audience lapped up like thirsty dogs.

There was so much to be admired in the performers. Their skill was second to none, defying gravity and even their own bodies to provide a thing of wonder for others to admire. But Anna knew that this wasn't why they were here. Not even the seated ones who had a few extra coins and thought themselves so much better. No, the truth was, they'd all come hoping to see something awful. They were the same sort of people who would have been entertained by public executions.

"One false move and the Flying Fairy will plummet to the earth, smashed to smithereens!" Gerrity bellowed, and the crowd drew in their breath as Lucy, her white-blonde ponytail streaming beneath her like a canary's wing swung higher and higher. All the time, building speed and momentum.

It was an apt description; at just seventeen, Lucy resembled a sweet fairy when her feet were on the ground. In the air, even more so, for her skill in the twists and turns was something of a miracle as she seemed to hover or fly at will.

Holding on with slim, fragile-looking arms, she rolled her body and let go to a gasp of the crowd. Tucking, she twisted in the air as strong and graceful as an eagle on the wing. There was not a sound as she turned and flew an impossible distance to the waiting trapeze that had been swung at just the right moment for her to catch. None of the crowd had noticed it before she grabbed hold and they let out a great sigh of awe.

Lucy's nimble fingers hooked on to the bar, and she unfurled into a beautifully neat, taut straight line as the complicated manoeuvre was complete.

The crowd breathed again, perhaps with a hint of disappointment.

Anna wondered if she were just a little jaded. Could you be jaded at thirteen? She'd been raised in the circus and knew nothing else, and she'd watched crowd after crowd silently willing catastrophe to do its worst. It had, of course, from time to time, and Anna had seen eyes wildly alight with mawkish glee even as the lips proclaimed the awfulness of the whole thing; the tragedy of it. But people loved tragedy. Tragedy was what they were paying to see whether they admitted it to themselves or not.

Of course, there was always tragedy, even if there was not an accident. For the most part, the tragedy displayed daily was the tragedy of birth. The deformed children who had grown up to discover that the only work on offer was to make a mockery of themselves and their lives as circus sideshows. For instance, the pinheaded man, his head so small that his body looked horribly wide. Anna felt her heart break every time she looked at him, yet all he ever did was smile. With his brain unable to develop within the constricted walls of so small a skull, he didn't have enough wits to know he was being stared at, mocked, and humiliated. Perhaps that was the only mercy in all of it.

Then there were the women with extraordinary facial and body hair. They seemed to be in constant supply, and she often wondered how it was Mr Gerrity found them. For the most part, the ladies didn't speak a word of English, and she'd never dared to ask where they came from. Circus men always seemed to be able to find the vulnerable; they had a sense for them, a natural talent for drawing them in.

"Our beautiful Flying Fairy lives to fly another day!" Mr Gerrity called out loudly. "But don't forget, we're here all week, ladies and gentlemen. Every day at the circus is different from the day before!" He always grew louder when he tried to tempt them back to spend their coins again.

Anna groaned inwardly. It would have been more honest of him to shout, *"Come back tomorrow, and maybe she really will fall next time!"*

Lucy had flown to the platform high above the crowd, stepping onto it as if it were on the ground. No nerves showed, there was no hint of anything other than the easiest balance. She let go of the trapeze and stood on the tiny platform. She looked beautiful in her skin-tight bodysuit. It was lilac and shone like silk, fine net wings attached to the sleeves, wings which flew when Lucy did. It was an outfit that would only ever be acceptable in the circus, not in the normal 1883; not in the England outside of the big top where hems were low and necklines impossibly high.

Lucy waved to the crowd; even that simple gesture was filled with balance and grace.

Anna waved back, knowing that Lucy probably couldn't even see her there. She waved because she was grateful; grateful for a few minutes of escape into a world where it was possible to fly.

"And now, the most amazing trick rider in England, the one and only Bernard Bailey!" Mr Gerrity roared, and the crowd let their attention wander away from the Flying Fairy as she climbed down the rope ladder to safety and prepared themselves for the appearance of Anna's father.

Even as Bernard Bailey flew out into the ring, the clattering of his horse's hooves loud enough to be heard over the musicians' sudden and wild playing, Anna turned away and eased back through the crowd and out of the big top.

Anna had prepared everything for the evening meal early that day and had only to warm it all through. She had a fire alight outside the high sided carriage that she and her father both lived and travelled in. Setting up a metal tripod, she hung the pan containing the rich stew above the flames.

Anna had already eaten her meal earlier, knowing that her father wouldn't care if she sat down to eat with him or not. The truth was, on the first night in a new town, Lucy was always too nervous to eat much as the night went on. Her sense of anxiety simply increased as she cooked and listened to the roar of the crowd inside the big top as they watched the amazing Bernard Bailey charging around the edge of the ring standing on his horse's back. She wondered if they would be so amazed by him if they'd seen how cruelly he treated his horses? If they knew what it took to make performers out of the poor creatures. She shook her head, she knew them, all of them, even though they'd never been introduced. She knew them well enough to know that they wouldn't care one way or the other. People who drew such pleasure from the very sight of the unfortunately born, the prospect of a woman falling to her death, or a beautiful wild animal forced to act against its every instinct, wouldn't care at all about beaten and broken horses.

"I saw you in the crowd today," Lucy said, walking towards her with a bright smile.

"Did you really?" Anna was amazed that a woman who needed every shred of concentration to work the trapeze could spare an ounce of it to look for the starstruck little girl who admired her so.

"At the end, when I was standing on the platform. I could see you waving at me." Lucy grinned and sat down on the grass beside Anna as she continued to keep an eye on the stew. "Making his dinner then?" she went on.

"Yes, I managed to get a little meat, so he should be happy for that much," Anna said and shrugged. She knew it was unlikely that her father would give her a word of praise about the meal she'd made for him. After all, she didn't get a word of praise for keeping the wooden carriage they lived in clean and orderly, his clothes laundered, his hair cut just the way he liked it, his chin freshly shaved. Surely, it would be easier to look after a baby.

"Are any of them ever happy about anything? I mean..." Lucy had begun conversationally, but her voice trailed away to nothing and Anna followed her gaze. She shouldn't have been surprised to see her father leaning one arm against one of the circus wagons, a young and adoring woman with her back against it looking up at him.

"It's always the same, Lucy. The first night in any town, he always picks up with somebody. I don't know how he does it; look, he's so much older than she is." Anna tried to bite back her disgust.

"Some women like it." Lucy shrugged. "It doesn't matter what he looks like or how old he is, for ten minutes he was the star of the show. I don't understand it myself, but women will throw themselves at any man at all if he was the centre of attention for a while, if all eyes were on him."

"I just wish he'd go somewhere else to... well..." Anna was too embarrassed to finish the sentence. Even though Lucy must surely have realised that Bernard Bailey's conquests were always made in the same little carriage where his daughter was trying to sleep, still, Anna couldn't admit it out loud.

"Why don't you come to me? Look, hand me out your blankets now before he gets here and come over to me as soon as you've finished feeding him. He looks engrossed enough, I'm sure he won't miss you if you sleep in my carriage."

"I'm sure he won't miss me either," Anna said sadly.

"I wish I hadn't said it quite like that, my sweet," Lucy said and put a long, slender arm around Anna's shoulders. "I suppose it's just the life we lead here, isn't it? Never settled anywhere, travelling all the way up the country only to turn around and travel all the way back down again. I suppose, in his own way, your father is lonely."

"I just wish he would go and be lonely in somebody else's carriage," Anna said and shuddered. "It's impossible to sleep when..." Again, she couldn't finish her sentence.

"This is a hard life, no doubt about it. I was born in a circus, Anna, just like you. Only, my father made me train as an acrobat and then a trapeze artist. There was never any choice in it, and he used to pick up women along the way. I understand how you feel," she went on in a soothing voice.

"You're so good at it, Lucy. Don't you like it?"

Lucy's eyes dropped to stare at the ground. There was a desolation about her that Anna had never seen before.

"I hate being here. I hate that I never learned anything else in my life but this." Lucy spread her bird-like arms, and for a moment, Anna thought she would fly away and hover before her like a fairy tale fairy. Of course, she didn't.

"You always look so content on the trapeze."

"It is the only time I *am* content. Being in the middle of the show, Mr Gerrity is not able to bawl and shout and throw things if he doesn't like what he sees. I forget they're all there; Gerrity and his wife, the crowd, everybody. It's the only time I feel free... when I'm flying. But then, like any captive bird, my wings are pushed back down against my body and I'm stuffed back inside the cage." Lucy's beautiful face looked so sad that Anna could have cried; her bright blue eyes, her impossibly pale blonde hair, everything about her so beautiful and for what? So that she could live a life without any choice at all.

"Come on then, hand down those blankets, and I'll go and hide them in my carriage. And come to me when you're ready, Anna, don't wait around," Lucy said, forcing herself to speak more brightly and kissing the top of Anna's head.

Read The Lost Nightingale for 0.99 or FREE with Kindle Unlimited

You can find all my books on Amazon, click the yellow follow button and Amazon will let you know when I have new releases and special offers.

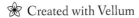 Created with Vellum

Printed in Great Britain
by Amazon